Refle
An As

8-91
D0832353

■

Macklin thought of everything in terms of death these days, a sure sign he had been in the business too long. For the first time in his life it was getting to be more than just a job. He couldn't watch the President speaking on television without thinking how absurdly easy it would bo to blow out his brains with a scoped rifle, bypassing the celebrated bullet-proof vest entirely, and be blocks away before the Secret Service reacted. When science announced a fresh victory over death, he thought only of ways to reverse the defeat.

■ ■ ■

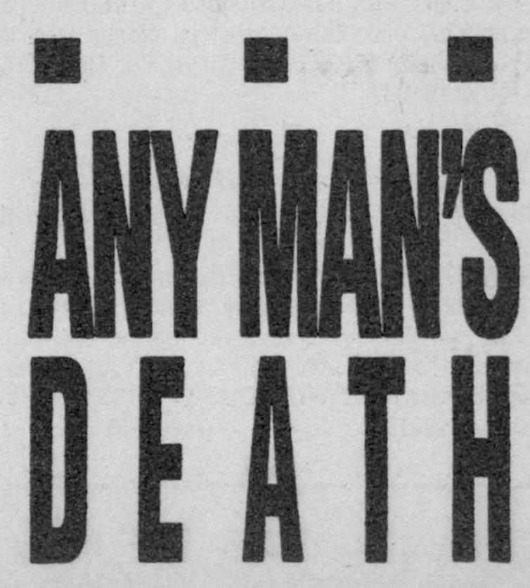

Other Peter Macklin Novels
by Loren D. Estleman

KILL ZONE

ROSES ARE DEAD

Published by
THE MYSTERIOUS PRESS

ATTENTION: SCHOOLS AND CORPORATIONS

MYSTERIOUS PRESS books, distributed by Warner Books, are available at quantity discounts with bulk purchase for educational, business, or sales promotional use. For information, please write to: SPECIAL SALES DEPARTMENT, MYSTERIOUS PRESS, 666 FIFTH AVENUE, NEW YORK, N.Y. 10103.

ARE THERE MYSTERIOUS PRESS BOOKS
YOU WANT BUT CANNOT FIND IN YOUR LOCAL STORES?

You can get any MYSTERIOUS PRESS title in print. Simply send title and retail price, plus $2.00 for the first book on any order and 50¢ for each additional book on that order, to cover mailing and handling costs. New York State and California residents add applicable sales tax. Enclose check or money order to: MYSTERIOUS PRESS, 129 WEST 56th St., NEW YORK, N.Y. 10019.

ANY MAN'S DEATH

LOREN D. ESTLEMAN

THE MYSTERIOUS PRESS

New York • London

MYSTERIOUS PRESS EDITION

Copyright © 1986 by Loren D. Estleman
All rights reserved.

Cover illustration by David McKelvey

Mysterious Press books are published in association with
Warner Books, Inc.
666 Fifth Avenue
New York, N.Y. 10103
A Warner Communications Company

Printed in the United States of America

Originally published in hardcover by The Mysterious Press.
First Mysterious Press Paperback Printing: September, 1987

10 9 8 7 6 5 4 3 2 1

For S.T.

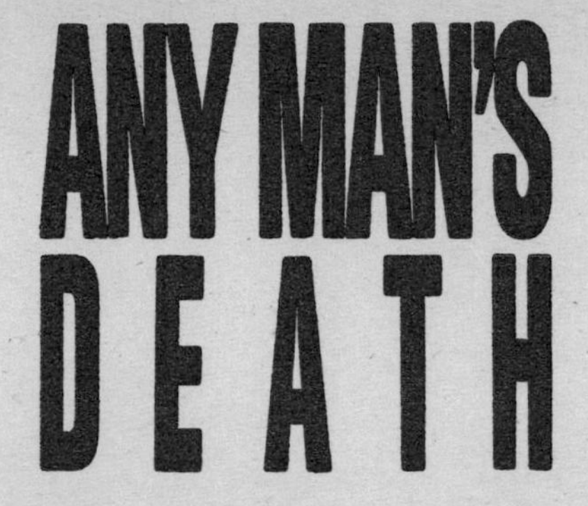
ANY MAN'S
DEATH

CHAPTER 1

Sister Lucinda was a quarter beat behind.

She was the only contralto in the group and its newest member, but the Reverend Thomas Aquinas Sunsmith flattered himself that he could have identified the responsible party in a chorus of sopranos. Before he got the Call he had played backup guitar with the Geeks out of Royal Oak, and he still had his ear, even in a crowd the size of the one he always drew for the late Sunday morning service when the Tigers were in town. He made a mental note to talk to the sister about it after everyone else had left.

When the singing was through and the parishioners had regained their seats, he opened the big Bible on the pulpit to the page he had marked with a guitar pick and began to read in the rich bass he had developed in those former days of darkness. In the Spartan interior of the church he was a startling figure wearing robes of rose-colored satin, a big brown man with a shaved head the size of a basketball against the sisters behind him in pale yellow with their hair in buns and the less noticeable four wide men in blue suits seated to his right. As he spoke he looked out on the congregation with eyes moist and black and strangely inanimate, like drippings from a black candle.

" 'Then the soldiers, when they had crucified Jesus,' " he thundered, " 'took his garments, and made four parts, to every soldier a part; and also his coat: now the coat was without seam, woven from the top throughout.

" 'They said therefore among themselves, let us not rend it, but cast lots for it, whose it shall be; that the scripture might be fulfilled, which saith, they parted my raiment among them, and for my vesture they did cast lots. These things therefore the soldiers did.' "

He slammed shut the book with a boom that reverberated in the rafters and made the audience jump. The basketball head swiveled slowly, leaving no seat untouched by the waxen black eyes as he came around from behind the pulpit with its lining of bulletproof plastic.

"I hate it when he does that," commented one of the wide men in blue to his neighbor.

"And so, dear friends," Sunsmith rumbled, "it remains to this day, that to gamble is a sin under the Bible and an abomination in the eyes of God; for he who wagers his chattel on the gaming table of greed is casting lots for the coat of our Lord on the cross, and will be damned for it."

Without taking his eyes off the audience, he reached behind the pulpit with one of the long arms he had used to lunge for C above high C and held up a sheet of paper.

"Brother Clark confiscated this from a man in Cadillac Square Tuesday morning. It is signed by an organization that calls itself Citizens for Casino Gambling in Detroit and claims to be a petition calling for a vote to legalize games of chance within the Detroit city limits. But this is not what it is, dear friends; no, indeed."

His voice rose. "It is a *pact*, not a petition, and it is not with your neighbors, but with *Satan*, and the CCGD does not stand for Citizens for Casino Gambling in Detroit, but for Cry Craps and Go to the Devil!"

This sparked cheering and appreciative laughter from the congregation. But Sunsmith was not smiling. He lowered the paper.

"Mind," he went on, more quietly, "that I do not speak against games of chance because they steal bread from the mouths of children, or because they reduce men and women to pigs snuffling in the trough; no, dear friends, these are not my reasons, although they should be enough for any decent man or woman. A government that smiles upon the casting of lots for Jesus' coat would as soon outlaw the Word of the Lord and cast us all into darkness. And so, dear friends, when the petitioner comes to your door and says that he represents Citizens for Casino Gambling in Detroit and asks for your signature on his pact, tell him that you will not cast lots for the coat of our Lord, but that instead you are casting your lot *with* our Lord, and if he still refuses to see the light, then show him the door! Three, four."

The sisters came in with "What a Friend We Have in Jesus," the sweet mix sliding over the cheering and applause in the congregation. But the effect was spoiled when Sister Lucinda entered the sixteenth bar a full beat behind the others. The Reverend Thomas Aquinas Sunsmith turned to glare at her, and in the act saved his own life. He saw the flash and felt something clip his collar and then he saw metal gleam and then all four wide men in blue were on their feet with their big nine-millimeters in their hands going off in ragged succession like four engines firing on a cold day. Big round spots like red quarters appeared on Sister Lucinda's yellow gown and her mouth opened and she dropped the gun and because her legs were covered she seemed to wither and shrink as the four guns followed her down.

The throb of gunfire in the big room took the place of the singing, and for an instant there was no reaction. Then a woman in the audience who had not seen Sister Lucinda falling saw the four wide men standing holding their empty guns with the actions run all the way back and the rest was screaming.

"Mr. Boniface."

The heavy man with the hooking features, sixty but black-haired and not a hair of it dyed because that wasn't allowed inside, barely glanced at the young sandy-haired man in the blue suit with orange pinstripes. Picante was with him in the corridor and the heavy man said, "Where's Klegg?"

"Tied up," Picante said. "This is one of the junior partners. Michael Boniface, Jason—"

"What the fuck I pay him for, he don't come down to see I get out when I'm supposed to? What if there was something wrong with the paperwork?"

The young lawyer said, "All the arrangements were made beforehand, Mr. Boniface."

"Bo-ni-*fa*-ce," corrected the heavy man.

The young man whitened. "Didn't I say it right? I—"

"Any way a punk like you says it, it comes out Boni*face*. Don't say it no more."

"Yes, sir."

They were walking down the corridor, which had an institutional smell of lemon wax and stationary air. The heavy man's suit, expensively tailored, was strained in front and his neck rolled over his tight collar. His face had a slightly bloated look.

Picante said, "You look good, Mike."

"Bullshit. That government food would blow up Gandhi."

They passed through the metal detector at the end of the corridor and crossed a narrow strip of grass to the paved driveway leading to the gate. There the young lawyer showed papers to the guard in the booth and the guard buzzed open the gate. A deep blue Mercury was parked against the curb outside. Picante opened the rear door and held it.

"Let the punk ride nigger," the heavy man said. "I got my fill of that shit between here and federal court."

The lawyer got into the back seat and the heavy man climbed in next to Picante in front. Picante was lean and dark in a textured brown polyester suit. He had long upper teeth and thinning brown hair that he combed sideways across his scalp and when he smiled, not often, his face broke into vertical creases like an accordion. The heavy man watched him transfer a nickel-plated Colt Diamondback .38 revolver from the glove compartment to his underarm holster.

"When you going to see my tailor?"

"When this suit wears out." Picante started the engine.

"You look like a fucking bag man. I'm embarrassed to be seen with you."

"So fire me." When they were moving Picante said, "You hear about that try on Sunsmith yesterday?"

"That asshole Maggiore." The heavy man pulled loose his necktie and undid the top button of his shirt. "When a sky pilot hands you grief you buy him. You don't ice him."

"It might not be Maggiore."

"He pulled everything out of narcotics and stuck it in numbers and then the Lotto came in and he got killed. Now he's sunk a million and a half in a shithouse load of tables and roulette wheels in Toledo and if they don't legalize gambling in Detroit and he brings the stuff in anyway he'll have raids up the wazoo. It's Maggiore okay. Cops got anything on the shooter yet?"

"Our guy there says no. Looks like someone hung a ringer in the choir."

"Gambling, shit. It ain't steady. Drugs, that's the growth industry."

"Draws fire, though."

"Three years I can do on my head. Did."

"Three years ain't what the judge gave you."

The heavy man said nothing to that. "Where's Macklin?"

"Around. Only he's freelancing now."

"Talk to him."

They spoke no more. It was a long drive from Milan to Detroit and Picante stayed off the expressways to show his employer some scenery he hadn't seen through his cell window. In Belleville a tan Buick Skyhawk slid up beside them at a stop light and the window on the passenger's side came down, leaking Tina Turner out into the open air.

Picante jammed his heel down on the accelerator just as the back seat window on the left side of the Mercury exploded. Wheeling one-handed around a panel truck crossing the intersection, he used his other to snatch the heavy man's lapel and pull him down across his lap. There was a second roar, but the Mercury was through the intersection now and buckshot struck the rear window and rattled down like a handful of dried peas. He negotiated three turns, clipping curbs twice and narrowly missing an old man walking his dog, and spun halfway up a grassy bank in a residential neighborhood before coming to a halt with gasoline walloping around inside the tank. In the rearview mirror he glimpsed the young lawyer levering himself upright in the back seat.

"You all right?" Picante asked the heavy man.

The heavy man sat up, patting himself all over. "Yeah. Who the hell taught you to drive?" He ran a hand back through his disheveled black hair.

"I've been shot!" exclaimed the lawyer.

Picante twisted around in his seat. The lawyer had a hand to his forehead, where blood was trickling through his left eyebrow. Picante grasped the lawyer's wrist and pulled the hand away. "You caught a pellet is all. Maybe a piece of glass. Lucky."

"Lucky? Getting shot is lucky? Oh, God, I'm going to be sick."

"Not in here." Picante unclipped the Colt Diamondback from under his arm, checked the load. A siren wound up in the distance. "That asshole Maggiore. He payrolls hopheads 'cause they work cheap. Sorry, Mike. I should of seen it."

"Sorry, hell. Just talk to Macklin." Grinning suddenly, the heavy man struck Picante's shoulder hard with the heel of his hand. "Jesus, it's good to be out."

He figured the two keys on the ring cost him thirty thousand dollars apiece.

Looking at the house objectively—the only way he looked at anything—he couldn't see where it was worth sixty thousand. Rust had perforated the gutters and the shingles were curling. There were more surprises inside, leaky pipes and a furnace that cut in only when some fairly determined individual fetched it a smart kick, but he had missed his second-floor study and any other house in the area would have run him as much or more. Even so, he figured having to buy it back from his ex-wife had cost him an extra ten in gall.

He was forty years old and the house was everything he owned, that and last year's green Camaro parked in the driveway. Other men his age were toting up the years between themselves and retirement. Most others in his line were dead or in jail. The rest, like him, went on working and trying not to think about diminishing returns. It was the only law they considered.

Working on not considering it, he inserted one of the keys in the front door lock and turned it. The key met no resistance and he stopped. He had locked it that morning.

He was forty and his reflexes were not what they had been. But they kicked in ahead of sluggish reason, and before the bare fact that the door was not locked had registered he was backing toward his car. He opened the door on the driver's side without turning his back to the house and got in.

"How are you, Mac?"

Peter Macklin recognized the lean dark man in the baggy brown suit sitting on the other side and relaxed. The man had one hand wrapped around a Colt revolver resting in his lap.

"Same old Picante," Macklin said.

"I slowed down some," said the man. "You too."

"Who's inside?"

"Couple of temporaries from Cleveland. Mike's casting his net wide these days. Maggiore's got this area fished out."

"I heard they were throwing him loose."

"This morning. Klegg sprang him a day early to beat the reporters."

"That's good."

"He's grateful, Mac. That was a hell of a thing you did for him on that boat. The feds liked it too and that's how come he's out as agreed."

"I didn't do it for him."

"He knows that. These days it's pay-as-you-go, no blood oaths or rings to kiss. He wants to see you."

"Tell him his invitations stink."

Picante looked down at the Colt as if he'd forgotten he was holding it. He didn't put it away. "Hell, Mac, it's been a couple of years. You don't keep track of your friends you lose them."

"I only carry when I'm working."

When Picante still didn't move, Macklin opened his corduroy sportcoat slowly. The other looked and returned the gun to its holster. "Mike's got work for you."

"I'm not connected now. He knows that."

"He knows a hell of a lot more than a lot of guys that didn't spend the last three years pressing the warden's pants. Like he knows you hire out."

"What's wrong with Cleveland?"

"You trust a Kelly girl to slam the back door, nothing else. There was a try on him this morning."

"I didn't hear."

"Cops, they sit on things they don't know what else to do with. He's okay; just mad."

"I remember you were pretty good."

Picante uncovered his long teeth. "My guts don't stretch that far these days. Besides, someone has to look out for Mike."

"Tell him thanks."

"He's paying fifteen thousand."

"It isn't that. I'm through popping people I don't know because someone else doesn't like them."

Picante touched his upper lip with the finger that had rested on the Colt's trigger. "The person he wants popped is Carlo Maggiore."

Macklin scratched his ear.

CHAPTER 2

Caroline Vetters, aka Lynn Venters, Cheryl Lynn, Carol Vintner, Paula Gaye—where'd that come from?—Carolyn Vetter, and Carole Ayn Vetters, was black and frowzy-looking, with a flat nose and beestung lips and welts under both eyes and a shaggy natural that looked tinted red in the black-and-white photograph. Priors said she had been arrested four times for solicitation for purposes of prostitution, twice for carrying a concealed weapon (served nine months in the Detroit House of Corrections the second time), once for attempted murder, charges dropped before trial. From front and side she might have been any one of a hundred women Inspector George Pontier saw lugging wash to the laundromat on Watson every day on his way to Detroit Police Headquarters; even he had to admit that a lot of black women of her age and station looked alike. And maybe it had nothing to do with race. Take ten bottle caps in ten colors and hit them all the same number of times with the same hammer and try to tell them apart. This particular bottle cap was thirty-six years old and wouldn't have to worry about being thirty-seven.

He looked up at Sergeant Lovelady's broad mealy face hovering over his desk. "What was the weapon and what did she use in the attempted?"

"Handgun, the CCWs," Lovelady said. "First one was German make, a real suicide special. She was lucky she got caught before she ever tried firing the thing. Other was S&W, a .32 with a history, only she was pulling ten days for solicitation the time it was fired into the ceiling at a stop-and-rob over by Ypsilanti. She used a sticker in the attempted, on her boyfriend. Allegedly," he added, deadpan.

Pontier wondered which was alleged, the attempted murder or the boyfriend. He put down the photo circular from Records and picked up the weapon recovered from the woman's body at the church. It was a Colt .357 magnum with nickel plating and an alligator grip. The serial number over the trigger guard had been cut out neatly in a rectangular piece with a jeweler's torch or something equally precise. He stroked the gouge with his thumb. "She came up in the world some toward the end."

"It's a pro piece for sure. A little loud."

"They like it that way sometimes. How they coming with the autopsy report?"

"Typing it up now. Lab says she had enough amphetamines in her plumbing to light up the Penobscot Building."

"Pump her up and shove her in shooting. Throw her away with the piece, there's plenty more where they came from. Christ." He stroked his moustache with an unselfconscious movement. He looked tall and slim even seated behind the desk, bald, with his graying fringe blown out professionally and light gray eyes that glittered in the varnished mahogany of his face. The commissioner liked his looks, and lately it seemed that he had appeared on the TV news more often than the mayor. "Sunsmith show yet?"

"Outside."

" 'Kay. You get an address on Caroline Vetters, run it in here. We find out where she went to the can this year and who with, I bet we turn up somebody connected."

"Dese guys?" Lovelady laid a finger alongside his pitted nose, bending it over.

"Them to start. And probably to finish. Christ, we were just getting shut of them and then this casino gambling thing comes along. Be a hell of a thing we let all these street soldiers run around popping each other over dope when there's another racket just laying around waiting for muscle. Anyway, taking Sunsmith out would shake up the organization against gambling. Who else if not dese guys? Shoo him in here."

He had on a lavender suit tailored out of a light soft material that hung like good drapery—a big man, six-three and broad enough to make an operation out of getting both shoulders through the door. His shaved head was shadowed like his chin. He took Pontier's hand in a palm that could wrap itself twice around the inspector's and lowered himself gracefully into a steel chair that creaked.

"Coffee, Reverend?" The inspector took his own seat behind the desk.

"If you have Sweet 'n Low."

Christ, he weighed three hundred easy. Pontier looked at Sergeant Lovelady, who turned and trundled out to get the coffee, himself almost as wide as Sunsmith but six inches shorter, firm and fat, with bowl-cut red hair and a complexion like rare hamburger.

"You hired Caroline Vetters?" started Pontier.

"She said her name was Lucinda. No, I didn't hire her."

Pontier hesitated. "At the church you said—"

"The ladies in the choir are not hired. They donate their time and voices to the service of God."

"They're not paid?"

"Ours is not a wealthy parish." He made a forlorn gesture with a plump hand wearing a large diamond. "She reported to practice last Tuesday when Sister Vernal was called away on a family matter. I've said that three times now."

"Sister Vernal told you she was called away?"

"No, Sister Lucinda did."

"You didn't check?"

He smiled for the first time, two rows of big teeth glittering like an old Buick grille. "You mean why didn't I suspect Sister Lucinda of lying to cheat the church out of peace and contentment?"

"You're a public figure, Reverend. Public figures have enemies. Especially those who involve themselves in local politics. You should know. We've tried to reach Vernal Brooks; her phone doesn't answer and no one's seen her since last Monday when she complained to her landlady about a stuck window. We checked out the apartment. Her clothes are there. No Vernal. I'm betting she's as dead as Lucinda."

"Then God rest her."

"You don't seem very upset."

Sergeant Lovelady came in then with the coffee and four packages of Sweet 'n Low. Sunsmith tore them open daintily with his big fingers and emptied all of them into the Styrofoam cup. "I don't know her that well," he said, dusting off his palms. "The devout life is demanding. Only a few can sustain it. There is a turnover."

"Any ideas on why Caroline Vetters tried to kill you?"

"The devil has pawns everywhere."

"How about threats? Received any lately?"

"Your men asked that already. Sister Asaul is bringing in the file."

"What's in the file?"

"Threatening letters, offensive telephone messages. Faith attracts nearly as much darkness as it does light."

"So does politics. Do you suspect anyone specific of the attempt yesterday?"

"Sister Lucinda acted alone. It's my regret that I was not

able to turn her from the devil's path before it was too late." The gesture this time was genuinely sad and oddly beautiful, considering his proportions.

Pontier played with a ballpoint pen, clicking the point in and out. "I can't help noticing that your faith isn't strong enough to exclude four bodyguards with permits to carry concealed weapons. You've got two former Detroit Police officers, a retired professional wrestler, and an ex-Lions tackle. What are they, apostles?"

"I'm told I present a large target. Darkness," he repeated.

"You've refused protective custody. Preventing the next attempt would be a lot easier if you were straight with me about who's trying to kill you and why."

The chair groaned as Sunsmith leaned forward, placing his great lavender-covered forearms on the desk. His candle-black eyes shone flatly. "God is a mystery with no one solution," he said. "Sometimes it's necessary to bargain with Satan in order to do the Lord's work. May I go? I have a fund-raiser."

Pontier nodded and placed his hand in the Reverend's paw as its owner rose with none of the noises a big man usually makes fighting gravity. The inspector said, "Sergeant Twill and Officer Ledyard will be joining your company, in plainclothes. The commissioner and I would be grateful if you didn't leave them behind in the confessional or something."

"My church doesn't believe in confessing."

The inspector bit back his reply. When Sunsmith had left, Lovelady said, "What's that mean about bargaining with the devil?"

"Only that the separation of church and state is a joke." Pontier inserted his pen inside Sunsmith's empty coffee cup and tilted it toward him. He hadn't even seen him drinking from it.

Al was the golden retriever's name. In spite of it, the dog

was an effeminate-looking animal, all long silken red-gold hair and narrow head and back and large dark glistening eyes like Sal Mineo's. Watching Boniface stroking the dog, Macklin found himself wondering who had really ordered the job done on Mineo. He didn't believe that prominent people ever wandered innocently into trouble. They paid people to do that for them. Sitting, the dog leaned all its weight against its master's legs. If Boniface stirred in the big easy chair the dog would go sprawling. Trust.

"You'd of visited me in the can if they let you, wouldn't you, boy?" Boniface was saying. "Sure you would. My fucking daughter only came twice."

Picante, coloring a glass of water with bourbon from the drink cart near the window, said: "She came other times. You wouldn't see her."

"She brought that prick she's living with. Guy makes jewelry for a living, you believe it? I don't mean he's a jeweler, he makes that turquoise Indian crap you see at all the street fairs. Wears tie-dyed shirts like it's still sixty-eight, for chrissake, and one of them little beards like Maynard G. Krebs used to wear. *Dobie Gillis,* you remember that show? The reruns were always on when that kike bastard Morningstar had paper out on me and I couldn't go out in the street. He respected the sanctity of the home, that Jew did, I'll say that. Not like these fuckers now, blow off the back of your head in your own living room with your kid on your knee."

As he spoke, he tightened his grip on Al's neck. The dog yipped and rolled its eyes over white at its master, who resumed stroking its fur gently. Al leaned back against his legs. Picante brought over the drink.

"I got to take this stuff slow," said Boniface. "I had a guard smuggling in Haig & Haig the first year but they fired him. My first wife must be spinning in her grave. Two years dry is longer than we were married."

Macklin sipped his highball and looked out the window

across from the sofa he was sitting on. That floor of the Pontchartrain Hotel presented a view of the skyscrapers downtown and beyond them of the housing developments spreading as neat as pieces on a board to the horizon.

Boniface said, "Klegg didn't want us meeting here, public place like the Ponch. But, shit, you won't get caught, and even if you do you'll just say you were here paying your respects. I trust you like I trust Picante there. We're family."

"Except Mac quit the family," Picante pointed out.

"Well, the prodigal son, then. What was he going to do, go on working for that fucking hunchback, after Maggiore hung out paper on him? I should of made Picante *capo* in my place," he confided to Macklin, "only that would of meant war in the ranks. Maggiore was senior. Who knew the little shit was going to turn over on me like he did?"

Macklin said nothing. Boniface's mouth had grown foul in prison. Macklin missed the quiet son of Alberto "the Pope" Boniface and his old-world manner. The present incarnation had been talking ever since Macklin had entered the suite.

Picante said, "The feds are moving in on Maggiore."

"Not fast enough. When the prick gets nailed I want it to be me holding the hammer. The hammer being Mac here. The can cost me my place in line. Mac's going to make room."

"I'm independent now. I said that up front."

"Business is full of wildcats. Specialization's got it by the balls. You want someone popped you got to know up front does he get a bullet in the head or a blowtorch shoved up his ass, and then you got to go down the list till you come to someone who specializes in guns or torches. You're maybe the last general practitioner in the business. Also I know you'll do it right, on account of your own score with Maggiore."

"He tried to have me killed. If I made a business of squaring things with everyone who wanted me dead I'd die of old age still owing."

"I wasn't talking about the contract."

Sunlight coming through the window found pouches in Boniface's otherwise puffy face and glistened unhealthily on his penitentiary pallor. He was looking at Macklin in a way nobody else had ever looked at him but one other person, now dead. But for Picante, who didn't have the look, Boniface was the only man living who wasn't afraid of Macklin.

"My ear's on the ground, even in the can," Boniface went on. "Your boy's a Maggiore mechanic. Pulled off a couple of touches now and he's not bad. Prick like the hunchback makes a plumber out of your son, it's like someone fucked your daughter in your own house, am I right?"

Macklin set down his glass with one sip gone. "The deal always was we stayed out of each other's personal lives."

"Fuck the deal. That went down the toilet when you quit."

"Your boy—Robert?" said Picante.

"Roger."

"He's a write-off. He's tasted blood and even if you get him out he'll be like a sheep-killing dog you got to keep chained up. Question is, does Maggiore get away with it?"

"You mean like an eye for an eye?"

"Revenge stinks for business." Boniface scratched under the dog's chin. "Quit trying to bring Mac's blood to a boil. You'll be all day breaking the crust. No. I'm just saying you might get a boot out of this one, on top of the money. I don't care how it gets done so long as it gets done quick."

"I don't work fast."

"Thing is, he has to be taken out before he takes out this nigger preacher that's so loud against casino gambling. You don't hit public figures. Press gets on the mayor and the mayor gets on the cops and then we'll have to start throwing good people to the wolves. You got to cut this kind of thing off at the source."

"Also you don't know anything about gambling and if Maggiore gets it legalized and nails down all the casinos you're out in the cold."

"Hey, I never said I was a communist."

Macklin picked up the highball. "The White House could learn something from his security."

"If it was easy I wouldn't of called you."

"It's worth twenty."

Picante said, "Fifteen's the offer."

"You got to understand Mac's situation," Boniface said. "Man just went through a divorce. Seventeen."

"No, it's twenty."

"You're not that good. I hate to say it."

"Get someone who is, then."

Boniface looked down at the dog. Al's red-gold head was resting on his knee, eyes reduced to white slits, and in that moment dog and master looked alike. "You're a bad boy, Mac. You'd do this one for nothing without being asked." To Picante: "Give him ten now. The other ten when Maggiore turns up in the long term lot at Metro Airport."

Macklin drained his glass and set it down. It would be his last drink for a while.

CHAPTER 3

The Reverend Thomas Aquinas Sunsmith's four bodyguards made Paul Ledyard feel small for only the second time in his life.

The first time had been when he tried out for the Lions and the equipment manager had strapped him into eight sets of shoulder pads before he found a pair that wasn't too large. At six-one and two hundred he had been the biggest man on his high school varsity squad and made all-state two years in a row, but when he took the field with the Detroit third string he had felt like an ant in a cricket hatchery. Weeks later, when he had recovered from his first and only skirmish with a right guard nicknamed Rhino, he had learned that his high school coach, a family friend, had called in a marker to arrange the tryout to demonstrate to Ledyard that pro ball was not for him. It had cost him two ribs and his classic profile. But he had gone on to college and now had in eleven years with the Detroit Police, the last two on the detective squad.

Sunsmith's men were as big as the Reverend himself, deep

and square in blue suits whose jackets would wrap twice around Ledyard with enough material left over to make a vest. Their aftershave was strong and the nine-millimeter Smith & Wesson semiautomatics they wore under their arms showed only when they stretched with their jackets hanging open. They seldom spoke in his presence. He wondered if they were any more talkative when he wasn't there.

It was his first babysitting job and it bored him worse than stakeout. Bodyguards saw a lot of waiting rooms; it occurred to him that people who had waiting rooms all had the same taste in magazines. He'd been all through the current *Time* and *Newsweek*, even the financial reports, for chrissake, had chuckled at all the pictures in *Gentleman's Quarterly*, and knew all the floor plans in *Architectural Digest* by heart. One place had had *Playboy*, neatly bound in stiff clear plastic, but all the pictures had been taken by the same photographer, who seemed to be turned on by those goddamn legwarmers that just broke up the long clean line of a woman's leg. *USA Today* was sexier. He had given up admiring the various receptionists behind their imitation wood-grain desks when they all started to look alike too in blonde hair pinned up and sprayed hard as horn and worsted wool suits and lacquered nails shaped like teardrops. They were always doing something back there, meaningless little movements, never looking up. He decided that being a receptionist was not much better than guarding bodies.

While he busied himself drawing these conclusions, twenty-two floors up in a new skyscraper in suburban Warren, Sunsmith was twelve feet away drinking lemonade laced with vodka on the sofa inside the main office. His suit today was green, with a thin purple stripe that picked up the deep bluish tinge of his skin. The glass vanished once it was inside his big fist so that when he brought it up to his lips and then replaced it in the little recessed area on the arm of the sofa with its contents half gone he appeared to have pulled off a magic act. The soft sheen in his moist black eyes brightened when the alcohol struck bottom.

"You mix a respectable drink, Mr. Constable. I don't think I've had that combination before."

"Thank you. It's my own invention. I call it a Yellow Boy."

Sunsmith nodded, his scalp catching the light. The man seated in the leather chair across from him was white—very—with blond hair so light it was difficult to tell where it stopped being blond and started being gray. He wore it short on top but brushed over his ears on the sides to conceal a slight tendency toward sails. His steel-rimmed glasses were tinted amber and he wore a beige sportcoat over a pale yellow shirt and canary tie. Yellow seemed to be his favorite color.

"I see you've made an addition to your company," Constable said.

"He's a policeman. It was either that or move my congregation to the chapel at the Wayne County Jail. The mayor wants to keep me alive."

"That's odd, considering you're on opposite sides of the casino gambling question."

"A martyr is hard to beat in an election."

Constable measured out an inch of smile and sipped at his own Yellow Boy. His office looked like a living room, with good abstract oils on the walls and floor lamps with soft white bulbs. The desk was parked in a corner by the curtained window; he never entertained from behind it. "How much this time, Reverend?"

"That's up to your conscience, Mr. Constable. Yours and your employer's. Did I mention that all donations are legally deductible?"

"Every time. I can't help wondering what you do with the money."

"The church needs a new roof and the youth center needs more room."

"I had your file pulled after you called for this appointment. We've made donations totaling sixty-three thousand dollars over the past fifteen months. That must be some contractor you're using."

"Faith is expensive."

"I can't help but suspect this firm is helping to finance your campaign against legalized gambling. Which I find counterproductive, seeing as how Charles Maggiore is our major stockholder."

"Has he complained?"

"Rather loudly. But he hasn't shut off your credit."

"*That* would be counterproductive."

"Not as much as you might think," Constable said. "True, we benefit from the return on investments logged officially as tax-deductible charitable contributions, and your church takes in more in collections than many secular businesses in which we hold interest. But we stand to gain far more if the gambling measure is passed."

"The police think Mr. Maggiore is trying to have me killed."

"We both know they're wrong. You don't invest in dead men."

"A record of his donations would be a handy thing to reveal when the police try to charge him with my murder," Sunsmith suggested.

"It might be, were there such a record."

"Well, *someone* is trying to free my soul."

"Just who that is is as much our concern as it is yours."

"I hardly think that. 'Life is real, life is earnest, and the grave is not its goal.' "

"Solomon?"

"Longfellow."

Constable ran a polished nail around the lip of his glass. "Is it at all unreasonable to ask you not to persecute the measure quite so energetically?"

"Gambling is a sin before God," intoned Sunsmith, not smiling. "My soul is not on the block."

"Mr. Maggiore understands that. It's why he trusts you to honor his investments even if they're off the books." Constable rose. "Will ten thousand take care of the roof?"

"I will ask the sisters to pray for him each time it rains."

"He'll be relieved to hear it." He went over to buzz the receptionist.

CHAPTER 4

The messenger was a young black man in a blue nylon Eisenhower jacket and red necktie with his hair blown out into a modest Afro. When Macklin opened the door, his visitor handed him the flat package wrapped in brown paper without a word.

"Cops are watching the place," Macklin said.

" 'S'okay. The service is legit."

The killer closed the door and carried the package upstairs to the study. Boniface had legitimate investments everywhere and even more businesses whose owners owed him favors. He doubted that the old man had had to pay for anything in years, not counting killers and lawyers. It was like him to arrange illegal deliveries by legal means in broad daylight. A paranoid like Maggiore would have set up an exchange in the monkey house at the Detroit Zoo or on a dock down by the river. Except Macklin would never have agreed to an exchange set up by Maggiore.

Inside the study he locked the door and drew the curtains over the window, then snapped on the desk lamp and tore the paper off the package. He noted with approval the unbroken seal on the two-toned pasteboard box, broke it, and used a pencil to pry the revolver loose from the Styrofoam molded around it inside. It was a Colt .38 Special, called the Shooting Master, mounted on a .45 New Service target frame. It was handsomely blued and the butt was equipped with checked walnut grips. For no particular reason he preferred the Smith & Wesson Police Special, but he went with whatever was available so long as it wasn't fully automatic and the caliber was neither too light nor too heavy. He admired the killers who made do with neat little .22s; admired them with no desire to emulate them. His marksmanship was good, not outstanding, and an inch this way or that with those small calibers could make the difference between a successful kill and life in the Southern Michigan Penitentiary at Jackson. Forty-fives and up were for water buffalo.

From the paper sack on the broad oak library table he drew a new roll of black friction tape, the kind with the rough surface that didn't hold fingerprints, and spent ten minutes taping the butt and hammer and trigger assembly. He always ditched the weapon at the scene, and gloves attracted too much attention in the balmy spring weather and were clumsy besides.

He laid aside the weapon and got up to unlock the file cabinet. The second drawer contained his income tax records for the past five years. Pulling out a thick manila folder labeled MEDICAL EXPENSES, he slid shut the drawer and relocked it and spread the folder's contents across the table. The display included several eight-by-ten color and black-and-white prints of a tanned blond man in his fifties with an athletic build spoiled a little by a hump on his left shoulder, a deformity he sought to cover through exquisite tailoring, with some success. Macklin, a polyester man, thought he would have done better to choose colors and patterns more conservative. But Charles Maggiore was not a conservative crimelord.

The blond Sicilian was a throwback to Capone days, not as loud or flashy, but closer to that type than he was to the gray Costellos and Genoveses and Gambinos of the middle years. His taste ran toward Jacuzzis and expensive health clubs and framed pictures of himself with an arm around Hollywood motion picture stars. He had started out as a street soldier for Boniface, survived several attempts on his life during the 1972 gang war, and worked his way up to stand in for Boniface while the latter was serving time for drug trafficking. The deal was that he would step aside when his predecessor returned. But the deal died the moment Maggiore's rump met Boniface's chair.

Among the other items on the table were a rundown of Maggiore's habits and associates, a complete medical history extorted out of a hospital resident with expensive weaknesses, and a floor plan of Maggiore's house in Grosse Pointe. Macklin had spent patient months compiling the information, slowly to avoid attracting his subject's notice, and although he knew most of it by heart he went through it one more time, making notes in a pad on the table to ram home the essential details. When that was done he read over his notes, then shuffled the neatly lettered sheets and photographs together with the pad, blank pages and all, and slid them into the wastebasket under the table. The weight of the items activated the electric shredder and in seconds the whole was reduced to tangled excelsior in the bottom of the basket. The device was one of the conveniences he had missed while his ex-wife was in possession of the house. The room's efficient soundproofing had been another.

He had spared two photographs. One was a telescopic shot printed in wallet size of a huge man with scarred brows and a broad square body sheathed in a black wool suit, holding open Maggiore's front door for its owner to pass through. This was Gordy, Maggiore's manservant and bodyguard. Macklin tucked the picture into the inside breast pocket of his sportcoat. The other was a newspaper photo of a smiling Maggiore in evening dress accepting the Rotarians' Man of the Year award. In it his face was barely larger than Macklin's thumbnail.

Macklin hoisted a large container of potting soil from the floor to the table and tipped it over onto its side so that the tightly packed contents faced out from the wall. Then he propped up the picture inside the lip of the pot, loaded the Colt from a box of cartridges included in the package, measured ten paces the length of the study, turned, and fired in one smooth motion.

The first shot obliterated Maggiore's face and filled the room with noise but not much smoke. "Smokeless powder" was an optimistic term, but he had fired some antique black-powder arms in the days of his apprenticeship and the difference between the thick, rotten-egg-stinking residue of those coarse grains and the cigarettelike haze caused by a modern self-contained cartridge was marked. The second shot took out Maggiore's right shoulder and most of the arm supporting the attractive plaque. The third left the Rotarian who shared the picture alone with a large hole.

Macklin stopped there. Earphones and earplugs during tests left a man unprepared for the gun's noise during the genuine event, and so he scorned them. His ears rang with the echo of the report contained by the room's six-inch cork lining.

The gun's heavy frame absorbed the recoil nicely, aiding accuracy. The potting soil stopped the bullets. Later he would dig them out and hammer them flat to destroy the striations and toss them into the garbage. Examining the photograph before consigning it to the shredder, he determined that the Colt fired a hair off to the left, but that was no problem. He intended to make the shot from as little distance as possible.

When, after twenty hours of labor, the same family physician who had delivered Gordy's mother freed a thirteen-pound boy from her womb, the doctor looked through the fogged lenses of his spectacles and instructed his nurse to tell the boy's father not to worry. "He's got a schlong on him like a black Angus."

Six years later the same doctor, almost bald then and growing deaf, put his hand on the boy's shoulder after his examination—reaching up to do it—and informed his parents that the problem was glandular, but that it could be controlled with drugs. By then he was the biggest child in school and taller than most of his teachers.

At age ten he was ducking through doorways, swiveling to clear his shoulders. Strangers addressed him as if he were an adult and came away thinking he was retarded. He wearied of always playing the Frankenstein monster with his schoolmates, but that problem solved itself when their parents forbade them to play with him.

By the time he dropped out of high school he had stopped growing, six feet eight and three hundred and twelve pounds of arrested physical development, a joke with a square brow and a prognathous jaw, a candidate for the Rondo Hatton lookalike contest, something the parents in his neighborhood used to frighten their children into going to bed on time. A promoter who had helped train Sonny Liston talked him into leaving school and going on the road, where he boxed small-town toughs and former heavyweight contenders on their way down. He took fearsome beatings and was disqualified several times when during clinches he cracked vertebrae and pulverized ribs. His opponents bounced their gloves off his kidneys and bared their teeth and wriggled and went limp as firehoses in his arms. One passed into a coma and was still on a life support system four years later. Gordy called the private hospital once a month to check on the man's condition. Part of his paycheck went regularly into the family's medical account.

The event sickened him on boxing. He tried professional wrestling, billing himself as Godzilla, but it was just as brutal for all the show business. He had already determined to quit when Charles Maggiore sent a man to Joe Louis Arena where he was touring with the Superstars of Wrestling to invite him to Maggiore's house in Grosse Pointe. Himself a dark man of Albanian extraction, Gordy stood in awe of the blond Sicilian in his sporty clothes and of the house with its bulletproof picture window looking out on the blue-glass surface of Lake St. Clair, but he felt a bond with this man whose congenital hump made him a fellow physical unfortunate. Maggiore said he had seen Gordy wrestle on television and imagined that he made a lot of money. His eyebrows twitched when Gordy told him how little. "I'll double it if you come to work for me."

Gordy hesitated. He had never heard of his host, but he couldn't miss the significance of the limousine in which he had ridden there with its thick tinted Plexiglas windows and of the men patrolling the grounds wearing jackets in eighty-degree weather. He had no intention of exchanging one heartless profession for another that involved breaking the bones of people who owed other people money. Maggiore sensed his reservations and quickly explained that his job would be to protect his employer from harm, nothing more. He would give Gordy twenty-four hours to consider the offer.

He spent that night on a walking tour of Detroit. The city reminded him a little of his native Philadelphia with its combination of gritty old Art Deco buildings and space-age plastic, and the lights of Windsor across the river enchanted him. Once, wandering over the ugly concrete covering the Wayne County Community College campus, he was accosted by a young black man in a Nike T-shirt who flashed a knife that was quicky put away when the moon came out from behind a cloud, grafting Gordy's huge silhouette to the surrounding architecture. "Evening," greeted the young man, fixing a grin on his narrow features. Gordy nodded and waited until he retreated into the shadows before continuing his own journey back to the hotel. He had decided to accept the job.

That was three years ago. Maggiore's confidence in his big bodyguard had grown to the point where he had dismissed most of his security and placed Gordy in charge of what remained, promoting him to majordomo in the process, with a raise in salary. He had gotten the giant a permit to carry a concealed weapon, but Gordy never used the gun; one glimpse of him in his neatly tailored black suit was enough to persuade the occasional hostile visitor to leave whatever weapon he had brought with him where it was.

Now he stood blocking the entrance of the Grosse Pointe house as efficiently as the door he had just opened, looking down from under the shiny white scar tissue on his brows at the slim bald black man on the front porch. It was evident from the way the man looked back that he wasn't accustomed to raising his eyes to meet anyone's gaze. He was six-two in a gray suit specially constructed for him, with a barbered moustache and gray eyes light in his very dark face.

"Inspector Pontier," he said, showing the badge in the leather folder. "I called earlier."

After a beat, Gordy moved aside to let him enter. The way the man had looked at him, he thought he had been about to ask him about the weather up there, the same dumb old shit. But it wasn't fear of consequences that had made him decide against it as it had been with some others, he was sure of that. Trying to scare a policeman was pointless; but it wasn't that either. The big man closed the door and escorted Pontier to the room his employer called the library and shut him inside.

Moving back up the hallway, Gordy decided it was Pontier himself who didn't scare. You met them sometimes.

Pontier made a show of looking around. "I don't see any books."

"Books? Oh. The library." Lowering himself behind the big bare desk in front of the bulletproof window, Maggiore spread the vent in his sunset-orange silk jacket to keep the material from creasing. A man made cautious by a number of contracts on his life, he had overcome his aversion to shaking hands long enough to clasp the inspector's. Now that Pontier was ensconced in the leather chair on his side of the desk he relaxed a little. "I hardly ever study anything in here, so it's not that, and the den sounds like the place where Mr. Cleaver had his little heart-to-heart talks with Wally and the Beaver. The office sounds too much like work. I'm thinking of putting in some books, but where?" He spread his hands, indicating walls covered with framed pictures, Maggiore with everyone but Caruso and Sarah Bernhardt.

"Why not call it the studio?"

"Studio. I like it." He folded his hands across his flat belly, swiveling to right and left. But for the hump he could have been a movie star who made all his money in the sixties and then retired. He sometimes told people he had appeared in beach pictures with Frankie and Annette, just to see their reactions. One woman said yes, she recognized him from a crowd scene. "Look, Inspector, I'll save us both some time. I didn't have anything to do with that try on Mike Boniface. Why should I? He's out of the running."

"Is he?"

"You wouldn't believe it, but prison's a worse stigma in our business than in most others. Lawyer goes up, a doctor, he gets a chance later to take back his license. Even politicians get themselves re-elected while they're in the holding tank. We're like first-generation legit and sensitive about it. He'd be lucky to land a slot machine franchise in Dearborn. If we were still running slot machines."

"I thought your business was corporate consulting."

"Yeah, and yours is security services. And public toilets are rest areas and TV weathermen are meteorologists but they still can't tell you what's going on outside their own windows. My mailman calls himself an information dispersal engineer, for chrissake. Boniface is stale news."

"Who said I was here about Boniface?"

Maggiore hooked his right arm over the back of his chair. The hump was less noticeable in that position. There were cops he liked and cops he didn't, and whether they were in his corporate budget had little to do with it: he liked some of the honest ones, too. But he didn't care for Pontier or this new breed of black, turned on a lathe and rubbed down smooth to slide into the white mainstream. In a few generations even the black would start flaking off. Aloud he said, "Who then, Sunsmith?"

"Let's talk about Sunsmith. Where were you at eleven o'clock Sunday morning?"

"Where I usually am at that time, reading Charlie Brown at the breakfast table. Ask Gordy."

"Gordy's the skyscraper that met me at the door?"

"I've got enemies same as you. You could afford one, wouldn't you hire a bodyguard?"

"I made forty thousand last year before taxes."

"That's just about what I *paid* in taxes."

"You want your part of it back?"

"Hey, I wasn't flexing any muscles." He took the arm down. "Inspector, I confess. I blacked my face and dressed up in drag and shot at Sunsmith myself. I didn't agree with his interpretation of the Old Testament."

"Caroline Vetters had a history of addiction to heroin and prescription drugs. She had five connections that we know of. Two of them are with the Boniface family. Now the Maggiore family."

"I'm not into narcotics. The heat isn't worth it."

"That's not what the DEA says. They're cooperating with ATF to see you go down on that charge of smuggling guns to South America."

"That trial hasn't started yet. You know where my cash is tied up."

"In the very thing Sunsmith is crusading against."

"Clergymen are off limits, especially famous ones. Same as cops and reporters and people in office."

"Nobody's off limits if Charles Maggiore wants him out bad enough."

"Shit. Look at it from my side. I take out Sunsmith, close his mouth, I open up the mouth of everybody in his congregation, swing everybody sitting on the fence over to his side and some that are on mine. A dead saint is a hell of a lot tougher to fight than a live clown in a pink robe. If I thought he'd accept them I'd fucking send some of my people over to see he doesn't slip while walking across the water in his bathtub and hit his head, because as sure as God's a Sicilian they'll say I slugged him with a roulette wheel."

Pontier was playing with his moustache. "You make a hell of a case. I'll say that."

"I'm telling it true and you know it."

"Of course, you could be working the double backspin. Kill the Reverend and count on everybody thinking you innocent because killing him would be worse for you than not killing him."

"Jesus Christ." The slick nigger even thought like a white cop. "He gets dead he gets dead, everybody knows why regardless of who ordered it. Either way I'm behind the eight ball."

"It's just the lady or the tiger with you mob guys, isn't it?"

"More like the tiger or the tiger."

"Well, don't leave town." Pontier placed his hands on the arms of his chair.

"You mean Grosse Pointe?"

"You know what I mean."

Sergeant Lovelady sat slumped in rolls of fat behind the wheel of the unmarked car parked across the street from

Maggiore's house. His favorite yellow blazer was bunched around his chest under his arms, the button fastened. Pontier thought he looked like the Michelin man. He got in on the passenger's side. "See anything?"

"That freak in the black suit came out once to chase biplanes off the roof. Where do they find guys like that, the circus?"

"You know Maggiore. The little guinea hunchback thinks he's Al Capone."

"You play up to it?"

"I had him thinking he was Public Enemy Number One, right behind Dillinger and Genghis Khan. It's worth it to watch him strut. Boniface was his, all right."

"That's Belleville's hot handle. What about Sunsmith?"

"No, somebody else wants Sunsmith. Maggiore's just the lightning rod." Pontier unbuttoned his jacket and rolled down the window. "Let's go back to thirteen hundred and make some phone calls."

CHAPTER 5

Sister Mercer thought the young man looked just like David Carradine.

She was a Carradine fan, going back to before *Kung Fu*, when he was still playing the wastrel sons of powerful ranchers on *Gunsmoke*; and tended to measure most men she encountered against that standard. (Not the Reverend, however.) This one had hair as long, except his was black, and he had the bone structure and sensuous lips and the lanky build under a fashionably faded blue velour sweatshirt with its sleeves pushed back past his forearms and jeans gone almost white from wearing and washing. But his eyes were more visible than Carradine's, not just slits, and he was considerably younger despite the shrunken look of his skin, his caved-in cheeks. She guessed he was in his early twenties. In fact he was seventeen.

She met him in the laundromat on the ground floor of her apartment complex in Dearborn Heights, where he said he was watching a friend's apartment until the friend returned from a business trip. The conversation started when he warned her that the machine she was about to load wasn't working and that she'd just be wasting quarters, try this one over here. They were alone in the room that smelled of soap and dank concrete. Normally she avoided contact with strangers under those circumstances, but this one was clean and polite and looked just like David Carradine. He asked her if she had plans for lunch. She said she had choir practice in half an hour. He offered to drive her and she declined. When her small load was dry he held the door for her and said he hoped he'd run into her again.

She had even island features and cocoa skin and if her hair didn't curl so tightly she might have been mistaken for Mexican. The corduroy slacks she was wearing that day emphasized her broad hips, and she was self-conscious about them. The only time she didn't feel that way was when she had on the yellow satin robe that fell in straight folds from her breast to the floor. Men in the congregation admired her when she sang with the others and quickly forgot about her when they saw her in street clothes. She had tried dieting, only to lose all her weight above the waist, and she hadn't the tenacity to follow an exercise program, although she had tried that too. She was thirty-four years old and had just about given up on male companionship.

So she felt a little leap in her breast when the young man, who said his name was Roger Martin, met her at the church door as she was leaving practice. He drove her in his spotless old blue Plymouth Duster to a restaurant in Greektown. That night he took her to dinner on the *Star of Detroit* and stayed with her in her apartment until dawn. The affair was on.

Three days later—five since Sister Lucinda had tried to kill the Reverend, but when no more attempts followed, Mercer had stopped counting them—she lay naked atop Roger in the dawn light gathering in her bedroom, nuzzling his hairless chest while he stroked smooth palms over her buttocks. He asked her what it was like to work for the church.

"The Reverend works for the church," she said. "I work for the Reverend."

"What's he like?"

"He's the most Christian man in the world."

"Well, it's his job."

"No, it's the way he is." She lay listening to Roger's heartbeat. "He doesn't pay any of us, we're volunteers. But he knows I'm on welfare and he gives me money sometimes. I never ask for it, and he won't take it back. He does it for some of the others too. That's the way he is. Most people don't know it, but he owns the Eternal Mercy missions downtown and in Redford. Everyone thinks he's rich, living off his collections; but he gives most of it away."

"He need any help?"

She laughed and kissed him on the lips. But he was serious. "Well, like what sort of help?"

"Man like that, people should be told about the good he does," Roger said. "It could double his collections. He could do twice as much good with twice as much money. See, I'm a human relations consultant."

"What's that?"

"Well, it's sort of my dad's invention. He's one too. It's like public relations, only softer. Not so much hype. A PR flack, if there's nothing good to say about his client he makes something up. A human relations man makes sure the truth gets out. It's more honest."

"I think I understand." But she didn't. She rubbed a palm across his right nipple, feeling it stiffen. In the gentle light he looked no older than seventeen. It had been a shock to learn she was twice his age. But it wasn't a sin, and it was a warm feeling, the thought that she could attract a good-looking young man, with teenage girls so brazen these days. "I don't think he'll hire you."

" 'Cause I'm just a kid?"

"You're not a kid." She kissed him. "But he handles his own publicity. He's good at it."

"Think he'll talk to me?"

"It won't do any good."

"You might be surprised. I'm a charmer." He ran his hands up to her shoulder blades and back down to her hips. She arched.

"I'll ask him," she croaked, straddling his narrow body.

Two hours later, after a shower and change, the young man whom Sister Mercer knew as Roger Martin left his apartment in Royal Oak to place a call from a public telephone outside a Michigan Bell office three blocks away. Waiting for his watch to read 8:35, he smoked his tenth cigarette that morning. He had taken up the habit when he'd kicked heroin. Now that his appetite was back and his nerves were settling into a steady thrum, he hoped to taper off tobacco before long. His father had narrowed his own weaknesses by giving up most of the vices, and since his father was still alive in a high-risk profession it seemed like a good idea. That he and his father hated each other was beside the point.

When the watch hands moved into position he snapped away the cigarette, fed a quarter into the slot, and dialed a number from memory. The telephone rang eleven times, twelve. He stayed on. On thirteen the receiver was lifted on the other end.

"This is Roger Macklin," he said into the silence.

There was a pause before a man's voice came on. "Make the delivery." The line went dead.

After a beat, Roger hung up, grinning. He went back to his apartment to rest. All this groundwork was cutting in on his sleeping hours.

The blue-black Cadillac salon model looked attenuated, a Warner Brothers cartoon vehicle that snaked around corners and followed dips in the road like a centipede. Its windows were opaque on the outside and when it slid into the curb in front of the racquet club on Gratiot it took up two full parking spaces. Macklin pulled his Camaro into a loading zone a block and a half back and watched through binoculars as Gordy unfolded himself in sections from the limousine's front seat and held open the rear door for his employer, shielding Maggiore entirely from Macklin's view with his body. All the killer saw of the Sicilian on his way across the sidewalk and up the front steps was a patch of blond hair and an elbow sheathed in bright expensive material. The two went inside, Gordy bending his knees and turning his hips to clear the doorframe.

What made the big man so desirable as a bodyguard had little to do with his size, Macklin decided. He would have taken a bullet or a bomb meant for his employer without hesitation. The fact was as clear as if it were painted on his billboard-size back. It was a formidable weapon at a time when even high-level bosses of Maggiore's influence were selling out their peers in return for government clemency.

Normally, Macklin gave little thought to bodyguards. They were just window dressing after all, a measure of a man's status. He remembered the numbers man on Antietam who had surrounded himself with wild-haired Haitians armed with machetes, Christ, *machetes* that they carried bold as cane-cutters down the street at collection time. They had terrified the neighborhood. But then Macklin had paid two of them five hundred dollars apiece to hold the others off with blades drawn while Macklin popped the numbers man in a vacant lot on his way to the condemned hotel where he conducted business. You bought them when you couldn't scare them off, and if you couldn't buy them you took them out with their bosses. But Gordy had no price and there was no predicting how many bullets his enormous frame could handle before he reached out with one of those hands that could palm a bowling ball and crushed his assailant's throat like a soda straw. Besides, Macklin liked him.

The killer waited. Less than two minutes behind the Cadillac, a green panel truck with a cartoon bee in a derby painted on the side cruised past and made a right at the corner beyond the racquet club building. Thirty seconds later it came back along that same cross street in the opposite direction, turned left onto Gratiot, and drifted to a stop by a fire hydrant across from the limousine. A magnetic sign reading BUSY BEE DIAPER SERVICE decorated the door on the passenger's side. Christ, a diaper service in the Pampers age. If anything the feds were dumber than they had been under Hoover. He could swear he saw the camera lens poking through one of the busy bee's eyes.

Waiting, he turned on the radio. Paul Harvey horse's-assed his way through the light moment at the end of his broadcast and yielded to the local news. Lightning had struck two teenagers playing golf at Oakland Hills, killing one and critically injuring the other. The badly decomposed body of a four-year-old girl missing for three weeks from her parents' home in Farmington had been found jammed into a culvert off Beech-Daly Road in Redford Township. The American Civil Liberties Union was working on a way to try a man a second time for a crime for which he had received a sentence the ACLU considered too light. The mayor was accusing a Republican of racism, or maybe it was a racist he was accusing of Republicanism; the announcer didn't seem too sure. Lightning never struck where and whom you wanted it to.

The station then played a taped excerpt from a speech delivered by the Reverend Thomas Aquinas Sunsmith at the dedication of a new free clinic in Taylor. Somehow he had worked in a reference to the temptations of Jesus by way of introducing his favorite subject, the casino gambling measure in Detroit. Macklin liked listening to his voice. If there was a God, he hoped He sounded like the Reverend Thomas Aquinas Sunsmith.

The light at the corner changed twice while he was waiting. It was just turning amber when a semi truck with a double bottom trundled past farting its air brakes. It stopped with its front tires in the middle of the crosswalk. Macklin turned off the radio and climbed out of the Camaro.

The huge truck was still waiting at the light, its diesel engine burbling, when Macklin reached the Cadillac. His view of the panel truck on the opposite side of the street was completely blocked. He slid a Slim Jim from his deep inside breast pocket, popped up the lock button on the door on the driver's side of the limousine in less than a second, and opened the door. The light had changed, but the driver of the semi was signaling a turn and had to let a string of cars pass through the intersection before he could ease out. By the time he released his brakes with a long hissing sigh, Macklin had finished and relocked the door. He was inside his own car before the panel truck's view of the limousine was restored. He started the engine, entered traffic, and swept past the Busy Bee without looking in that direction.

When Gordy escorted his employer out of the building forty-five minutes later—Maggiore's hair still damp from the shower following his workout—he spotted the panel truck and thought, dumb feds. He closed the Cadillac's rear door on Maggiore and compacted himself into the driver's seat. With the key halfway to the ignition he froze. A photograph of himself holding the front door of the house in Grosse Pointe for Maggiore was secured with a pin to the horn button in the center of the steering wheel.

He unpinned it and turned it over. On the back, someone had blocked-printed two words in black Magic Marker:

THAT EASY

CHAPTER 6

Elizabeth, Carmen Thalberg's black maid from the Central American republic of Belize, greeted the Reverend with a broad smile and accompanied him to the backyard patio, where her mistress lay sunning herself in a white bikini on a flowered chaise near the pool. The four corners of the pool were anchored by Grecian female nudes done in limestone—none of which, the Reverend decided, had anything on the fine slim lady in her late thirties offering her slick legs and flat belly to the sun. She had loads of light brown hair that looked golden out in the bright open and slender feet ending in neatly rounded nails without polish and around her neck was a tiny silver chain with crucifix attached. She didn't stir as Elizabeth left and the big black man moved a patio chair into the shade offered by the junipers that surrounded the yard and trusted his weight to it. His suit that day was teal trimmed with gold buttons and his tie and shirt were silver.

When after a full minute she still hadn't moved or spoken, he drew a thick envelope from inside his jacket and leaned forward to lay it on her stomach. She smiled then, teeth showing blue-white against the tan on top of her natural dark pigment, and sat up slightly to riffle long fingers through the bills inside. She had pale lashes behind the rose-tinted lenses of her big sunglasses. The Reverend wondered again about her ancestors.

"Five thousand," he said. "I could've sent someone, but I like your smile."

"Bullshit. You like my tits and ass. You know I'm always out by the pool this time of day. But thank you." She put the envelope and its contents on a metal table supporting a tall glass with lumps of ice in the bottom.

Her accent was faint, left over after years of voice coaching, and could have been mistaken for western or deep southern but for her Hispanic first name. The Reverend knew only that she had come out of Honduras or Guatemala or someplace like that, brought back by the son of a family that had made its fortune off an improved fuel pump design for General Motors. Shortly after their honeymoon the son had been kidnapped by Italian Marxists while touring a plant in Florence, and although the family paid the ransom his bloated body was found two days later floating down the Arno. He had left Carmen sixteen million dollars and two houses. The other was on Mackinac Island.

"Where are the Pips?" she asked.

"Outside. I'm safe enough here."

"Who's trying to kill you, a disappointed investor?"

"Are you disappointed?"

"I have five thousand dollars on my patio table."

"Maybe you want to turn some of it back," he said. "Sweeten the pot."

"Ask me next week. I'm expecting a dividend check from the offshore fields in Nova Scotia Monday."

He shook his big shiny head. "Rich people, they never seem to have any money."

"Rich people don't need it. Not the taxable kind, anyway."

"Not your rich. Music rich got to put up cash every time. I knew a man, he made more than you're worth off just one album. Whenever he checked into a hotel he had to pay a damage deposit up front. Well, he ate live mice onstage."

"Hotel people are so unreasonable."

He sat back, the legs of his chair spreading under him. "Collections are up. I can offer you the old scale until Wednesday. After that . . ." He turned up his palms.

"You'll offer me the scale we agreed on whenever. IRS finds out you're running in the black they'll yank your non-profit status and audit you back to the Carter administration."

"You too. Unless you've been declaring that." He waggled a finger toward the five thousand.

She took off the sunglasses. Her eyes were startlingly dark against the pale lashes. "How many investors does your church have?"

"I prefer to call them donors."

"Answer the question."

"It's a question you don't get to ask. You hire a band you like, you don't ask them did they study at Julliard or Joliet."

"Cut the music crap. You've been out of it too long. I find out you've been selling more than a hundred percent of your operation, paying me out of someone else's investment, I'll shut you down. The government can sting me on account of that's what it does and I have to take it. I don't have to take the old pyramid game off a broken-down guitar player with a pink Bible."

The accent was stronger when she was angry, not that she appeared angry otherwise. She didn't raise her voice or spit words; if anything her tone was more level than usual. But she bit off her consonants.

He said, "You lack faith."

"I was helping my brother sell maps to Blackbeard's buried treasure to gullible *turistas* when you were still learning your chords. You can't con a con."

"I thought maybe you married a suspicious man."

"Marty had modern ideas about involving wives in the business. He got my feet wet. When he died I got wet all over in a hurry."

So did Marty, he thought. "He needed God."

She touched the crucifix at her throat, an automatic gesture. "He had God. I have God. The place where I grew up, you still had God after you saw what the priests did in His name, you had Him for life."

"You feel that way I'm surprised you donate."

"Business can't be anything but business. That's another thing Marty taught me. His family didn't make three hundred million dollars avoiding doing business with people they didn't like."

"Sister Carmen," he said.

"What?"

"I was just thinking, you'd look good in yellow. Can you sing?"

"Like a brake. Am I supposed to be flattered or what? You ask me to join your harem."

"The choir sings for God. Only for God." It was his pulpit voice. "I serve the Lord, Who provides. Sins of the flesh committed under His roof are mortal."

"Save it for the congregation." She settled the glasses back on her nose and closed her eyes, lifting her chin to the sun.

For a moment he sat motionless. Then he leaned forward again and placed a huge palm on her oiled thigh. "I will ask the sisters to pray for you."

She opened her eyes to look down at the hand, then across at him. "He is risen."

Grinning, he withdrew the hand and got up to leave.

More junipers screened the front of the four-acre Bloomfield Hills plot from the street, where two cars were parked with their finishes baking in the sun. Two of the Reverend Sunsmith's personal bodyguards sat in the white-over-maroon Buick Electra in back while Paul Ledyard shared the cream Lincoln Continental stretch in front with the other two. The engine and air conditioning were off, and seated four feet behind them on the lavender-upholstered back seat he could smell the pair sweating under their aftershave. It was almost as bad as the locker room at headquarters.

He knew who belonged to the low sprawling white brick house behind the junipers. Two years before, he had accompanied a lieutenant named Wurmser to that address to ask Mrs. Thalberg to come down and identify an Italian national awaiting extradition back to his country for subversive activities. Wurmser had handled liaison with the authorities in Rome following her husband's kidnapping and had a bug up his ass about anything Italian if it could get him inside a trim pair of pants. Of course she couldn't match the prisoner's voice to the man with whom she had discussed ransom over the telephone, but Ledyard had thought the whole thing worthwhile for the opportunity to observe the handsome brown woman with the light hair and model's erect posture. Rich widows were always attractive in the newspapers but hardly ever were, really. This one fit the image. He wondered if she and the Reverend had something going.

But then the bushes shook a little on either side of the flagstone path leading back from the sidewalk and the great man inserted his shoulders between them, ducking a little, and the bodyguard behind the wheel of the Lincoln got out to open the rear door for him next to Ledyard. He had been in the house just under fifteen minutes; if they did have something going he was one fast man with a zipper. The whole seat dipped as he sat down.

"Church," he told the driver, when he was back behind the wheel.

As they slid away from the big house, the Buick following, Sunsmith's attention remained on the scenery gliding past the tinted windows. His right arm rested on the window ledge with the big diamond sparkling on his pinky. In the six days Ledyard had been babysitting him he hadn't said three words to the officer. They had spent a good part of that time on the road, stopping at residences and businesses throughout Detroit and most of its many suburbs. After the second day Ledyard had begun keeping a record of the stops in his pocket pad, writing them down from memory after his shift was over. He wasn't sure why. But he planned to discuss them with Sergeant Twill that evening when Twill came on to relieve him.

CHAPTER 7

The Arab was a perfect miniature of a grown man, less than five feet and eighty pounds and built to scale. He had plainly bought his silver-yoked cowboy shirt and brown corduroys in the children's department and could have been mistaken from behind for a boy of nine or ten. But his face with its pompadour of curly black hair was long and narrow, beveling back from a perfect wedge of a nose, brown, and pockmarked like wormwood. His eyes were dead yellow. Later it would occur to Roger that he was the first Arab he had ever seen without a moustache.

From behind the glass counter of the liquor store on Woodward, the man looked at his customer a long time before he turned and went through the door marked EMPLOYEES ONLY at the back, moving his chin for Roger to follow. It was a storeroom stacked almost to the cobwebby ceiling with cartons labeled Seagram's and Jack Daniel's and Old Granddad and a lot of other brands the young man didn't recognize, some of them identified by strange characters that looked like Hebrew although he was plenty sure it wasn't. The air was a hundred proof. He went on following the Arab through a square arch and down a flight of wooden stairs worn hollow, ducking to avoid a bare lit electric bulb under which his guide had passed without taking any such precautions.

In the basement were more cartons, empty, and a scabrous steel desk from a service station with bills and receipts arranged neatly on it in piles. The light came from another naked bulb that swung from its cord after the Arab pulled its chain. There was a rectangular window at ground level but it had been painted over.

In the center of the room, effectively filling it, stood an old oilburner in gray sheet metal with square ducts radiating out from it like spokes in a wheel. Bending, the Arab slid a Four Roses carton from the space between the furnace and a water heater of similar vintage. From this he drew a number of glassine bundles clouded pink with Cosmoline and laid them side by side on a bare corner of the desk.

Roger said, "Jesus, the furnace kicks in it'll blow the roof off the building."

"It hasn't worked as long as I own the place," said the Arab. "Besides, I don't keep ammunition down here. You have to deal that somewhere else."

Roger lifted a greasy rag off a control switch sealed with rust to the side of the furnace and unwrapped the bundles, using the rag to lift out their contents and inspect them. The light glistened off the Cosmoline-streaked surfaces of a Smith & Wesson short .44 magnum and a P-38 with a grip slim enough for a woman's hand and a nickeled High Standard .22 he didn't much like because it was a single-shot that you broke like a shotgun to replace the spent cartridge. He passed over a bulky bundle whose length suggested a Colt Python—too big—and slid out a Colt Woodsman .22 semi-automatic, the target model.

"That's an old one," the Arab said. "You won't find

another one off the NRA range. It came in the box, unsold stock from a guy in Texas that died. I bought out his widow. Ink was still wet on his obituary."

"No history?" Extending his right arm, Roger sighted in on a fat brown spider crouched in its web in the corner of the painted-over window.

"Was still in the box like I said. Three-fifty."

"Shit, downtown it wouldn't run me a hundred."

"Sure, score it off some nigger on Michigan Avenue, it's been used in a dozen stickups, killed a Stop 'n' Rob owner in Sterling Heights. Like carrying around a lit stick of dynamite till the cops toss you. Or deal it over the counter in some hock place, do the paperwork, cops trace it from ballistics straight to your pocket. I never sold nobody a piece with a pedigree."

"Yeah, I'd say that too I wanted to score a fast three and a half."

"Man, I don't have to do business with you. You came here."

"Give you three."

"Put the piece back. Nine years I been doing this, I got two arms and legs and I don't talk in a high voice. What's that tell you? I tell you what it tells you, it tells you I never sold out a customer. I don't haggle neither. Three-fifty is what I said and three-fifty is what I said."

Roger laid down the weapon and skinned seven fifties off a thick fold he took from his jeans pocket. The Arab accepted them and poked them through a slit shaped like an arrow in his cowboy shirt. "Get you something to carry it in," he said.

Back in his Royal Oak apartment, Roger lifted a stack of shirts and undershorts out of a drawer in his dresser in the bedroom, pulled up the false bottom, and put away the gun and a box of .22 shells he had bought elsewhere. Before replacing the panel he took out an unlabeled videocassette, which he carried into the small living room and fed into the VCR he had rented from a place in Birmingham.

"... It is a *pact,* not a petition, and it is not with your neighbors, but with *Satan,* and the CCGD does not stand for Citizens for Casino Gambling in Detroit, but for Cry Craps and Go to the Devil!"

Perched on the edge of a hassock with his elbows on his knees and his fists supporting his chin—the position in which he used to watch *Hawaii Five-O* when he was eight—he watched the big black man with a shaved head the size of a basketball strutting across the platform at a downriver dedication ceremony of some sort, his white satin robes shimmering in the sun. Roger had taped the open-air event off last night's *Six O'Clock News.* He knew well enough what the Reverend looked like, but wanted to get some idea of his security following last Sunday's attempt on his life.

He saw the four bodyguards in blue suits balancing out the sisters in yellow on the other side of the platform and a slightly smaller black man in a tan poplin jacket seated with them who was obviously a plainclothes officer, and when the camera swept briefly over the crowd cheering and applauding Sunsmith's sermon and swaying to "Jesus Loves Me," he spotted four more men wearing jackets in the heat. At least two of them were carrying walkie-talkies.

Cops were dumb, always preparing for the attack that had already taken place. They figured if someone had tried to kill someone else in public, that's how it was going to be the next time.

He was rewinding the tape when his telephone rang.

"Roger? It's Mercer."

He caught himself wondering for a bare instant how she could be calling him when he had just seen her singing on television with the rest of the choir. "Hi, babe," he said, stopping the tape. Onscreen, the Reverend posed with his mouth open pink and one arm raised, the robe sleeve slipping to expose a ruby cufflink. A wavy line crawled across his broad middle.

"I talked to him."

"Who?"

"Who. Him! He'll see you after the early service tomorrow morning."

Roger looked at the black eyes glaring back at him from the halted tape. "Alone?"

"Well, as alone as he gets."

"Okay," he said. "Thanks, babe."

There was a pause on the other end. "Will I see you tonight?"

"Tonight? Sure. It'll have to be a short night, though."

"Right. You're getting up early."

He said he'd stop by her apartment at six and they said good-bye. He started the tape again.

"It is a *pact*, not a petition, and it is not with your neighbors, but with *Satan* . . ."

Macklin felt tiny and exposed standing atop the pedestrian walkway over Grand River Avenue, outlined against a mauve sky with cars swishing below towed by the beams of their headlights. It was the kind of place a bodyguard would choose to meet someone—public, with both parties at an equal disadvantage. To the east rose the vertical scape of downtown, the turreted structures of the twenties and thirties pointed with the lights of the pyramided windows while the newer buildings showed square and flat, their glass sides lit in horizontal rows like characters on a computer screen. Westward stretched the tract homes and low-slung businesses of the suburbs, hugging the earth, illuminated headstones in the vast cemetery of the latter third of the twentieth century.

He thought of everything in terms of death these days, a sure sign he had been in the business too long. For the first time in his life it was getting to be more than just a job. He couldn't watch the President speaking on television without thinking how absurdly easy it would be to blow out his brains with a scoped rifle, bypassing the celebrated bullet-proof vest entirely, and be blocks away before the Secret Service reacted. When science announced a fresh victory over death, he thought only of ways to reverse the defeat. He wondered if carpenters went around studying woodgrains during their off hours. He wondered if they would worry about it if they did.

The walkway shifted slightly. Someone had mounted the steps, someone heavy. Macklin fingered the Shooting Master in its clip on his belt with his jacket hanging over it. He never carried a gun unless he was working or someone made an appointment to meet him in a place like a pedestrian walk-way over a busy street.

The newcomer rose into view thirty feet away at the top of the steps, a great bulk blotting out the lights behind him. The white V of his shirt cast a ghostly glow against the black of the rest of his attire. He came toward Macklin with an oddly graceful, gliding gait, like an Olympic skater. Or a professional wrestler.

"You don't need that, Gordy." Macklin tipped a hand toward the gun enveloped in the big man's right hand.

Gordy stopped walking, but left the gun where it was. "What was the idea of that picture?" he demanded.

"I didn't think you'd come when I invited you otherwise."

"I almost didn't then. You know Mr. Maggiore's phones are all tapped."

"It's why I let you call me back from an outside phone. Pick up any tails?"

"One. I lost him in the bus block on Woodward. What's it about?"

"I drew the contract on your boss."

"I guessed that. Just because I'm big don't mean I'm dumb."

"It's just business. Your boss started it when he hung out paper on Boniface."

"You're working for Boniface. I guessed that too."

"Well, you know enough about the way I work to know Maggiore's as good as in the box."

"He ain't so easy and you know it. He came up hard, not like those business school shits in New York. Maybe you're figuring on that and it's why we're meeting. Knock me down, clear the way."

"Gordy, if I wanted to do that I could've picked you off when you came up those steps. But you did me some turns back when we were on the same team and I owe you walking-away time. Don't go back tonight. Leave your stuff there and keep walking."

"Shit. You dragged me clear out here to tell me that? Shit."

"I'll blow you both down if you stick."

The dying light made pale squares of Gordy's scarred brow and cheeks and shadowed chin. His eyes were lost in hollows. "I'm a bodyguard. I guard the body. You blow one down you blow us both down. I guess we're through talking."

"I guess we are."

"Question is, do I get down from here without carrying any scrap metal I didn't bring up with me."

"Gordy, you know me better than that."

"I don't know you at all."

Macklin let out some air and raised his hands, locking them behind his neck. Holding his gun close to his ribcage, the big man stretched out an arm as long as one of Macklin's legs, patted him down, removed the Colt .38, clip and all, and hooked it on his own belt. Then he continued his search down to Macklin's ankles. Finally he straightened.

"I'll leave yours at the bottom of the steps. You'd just go out and buy another one."

"Next time I come shooting. Sorry, Gordy."

The big man flexed his fingers around the gun he was holding. "Maybe I kill you now."

"You won't."

"What makes it I won't?"

"A guy in a coma in a hospital back east that takes a call from Detroit once a month."

"Where'd you get that?"

"I do my homework."

Gordy said, "Shit," turned around, and lumbered back down the steps. The walkway went on swaying until his weight left it.

Macklin waited, watching the traffic sweeping under his feet, letting up a little now as rush hour drew to a close. He wasn't so sure Gordy wouldn't reconsider his humanitarian impulse and wait to pick him off as he descended. Macklin wondered if the big man really believed he had asked him out there to persuade him to stay out of the line of fire.

By the time the killer felt it was safe to go down he decided he did believe it. Gordy was smart, but his brain moved in a direct line. Just as an example, the Shooting Master was waiting in its clip just where he said it would be.

CHAPTER 8

"You should've killed him when you had the chance."

Steam drifted in front of Charles Maggiore's slightly lop-sided form, blurring it. He sat naked on the bench in a former half-bathroom that he had converted into a sauna, a man well muscled for his age but showing a stubborn ring around his middle and a cruel hump on his left shoulder with skin stretched over it. He was tanned but for a pale stripe around his hips and a bent white scar four inches long riding the top of his pelvis on the right side where a bullet had sliced across it in a botched attempt a dozen years before. It might have been an appendectomy scar.

"You pay other guys for that. We talked about this when I came to work for you." Gordy stood sweating on the tile floor, his suit turning darker. He made no move to wipe away the perspiration or otherwise show that he was uncomfortable. "What I can't figure is how come he told me at all. I don't buy that about not wanting to go through me to get you."

"Can't you?"

Gordy waited, but the blond Sicilian didn't supply the answer. "So what are you going to do?"

"I'm going to finish my sauna and turn in. You're going to get Phil Constable on the phone, tell him I want better guys. Those other two blew it big on Boniface."

"It's Saturday night. He won't be in the office."

"Fuck do I care? Get him at home or wherever he hangs out. Tell him I want that greaseball on a tray by morning or he'll be on one by noon. I don't have to tell you to use an outside phone."

"It won't stop Macklin. He'd spliff you just to watch your eyes roll back in your head."

"We'll both worry about Macklin. Me because he's got the paper on me, you because I pay you to worry about things like that. Meanwhile I don't close down the show just because I'm in season. I've been there more times than I've been out."

"Anything else?"

"Yeah. Lay out my green plaid and make sure the seven-millimeter is cleaned and loaded."

"It ain't registered. Feds toss you and find it they'll call in the locals. While you're pulling a year for CCW they'll be busy throwing up a stone case against you on all the other charges."

"I got lawyers to tell me that. They're worth shit to my ashes if Macklin gets past you. Gordy?"

"Yeah."

"Aren't you hot as hell in here in that suit?"

"The ring was hotter."

A drop of sweat quivered on each of Maggiore's eyelashes. He looked at the big bodyguard through them as through a prism. "You're sure you're not Sicilian? Maybe way back on your mother's side."

"Nope. French and Hungarian."

Maggiore told him to go make the call.

Later, in his dressing room trying on the lime-colored windowpane blazer, Maggiore peered objectively at his reflection in the full-length mirror, searching for some sign that betrayed he was armed. There was none.

Tailors who could design a jacket to cover a gun were becoming rare. Most executives of his stature preferred to pay others to carry weapons for them. Some of them would be dead in a year. They came straight out of business school and thought that because they wore rep ties and balled their pretty secretaries at lunch like any good Merrill Lynch broker they were in a legitimate line of work. But the business still depended on pimps and hookers and addicts at street level and a bullet was still the most effective means of getting the promotion list moving.

Why anyone wanted to move up was beyond him. The feds called him a crimelord when they weren't going partners with him and had hot pants to get him in bracelets on the *Six O'Clock News*. Most of the street talent was like the turkeys who had dropped the Boniface hit. When you did find a professional, sooner or later he turned. The business was Constable people on one side and Macklins on the other, with the Maggiores sitting between them with flanks exposed. All this on top of the usual problems with organized labor and with stockholders, the stockholders in this case being those dinosaurs in New York and Vegas who were still sorting out their wins and losses after the hits on Dutch Schultz and Bugsy Siegel. When it came down to it the only things you could count on were slim seven-millimeters and good tailors, and both were getting hard to find.

Macklin, parked across the street from Maggiore's house, was grateful when Gordy left to make the telephone call. The only car he had been able to lift that night with his limited knowledge of locking transmissions had been a red Nissan, and the seats in most foreign cars had been designed for young men with durable backs.

Gordy never left the house except to place calls for his boss that couldn't be trusted to the tapped lines on the premises; the meeting with Macklin had been a special event. While compiling his file on Maggiore, the killer had followed Gordy on several of these errands and learned that he had a favorite public telephone in the lobby of a restaurant in downtown Grosse Pointe. It was a twenty-minute round trip. The call itself would not last more than five minutes, as Gordy was not a gab. It was more than enough time.

He held no illusions that Maggiore would not see through his strategy in telling the bodyguard of his plans. The Sicilian's brain was Byzantine, forever wondering if the pea that had been discovered under the right walnut shell was now under the left, or if the man in charge of the game had counted on his thinking that and placed it under the right yet again, or if, thinking that his mark would be thinking just that, had instead placed it under the right on the theory that the mark would think that too simple. If A wants to kill B by fooling B into sending his bodyguard out of the house, it was in B's best interest to do just that and lay a trap for A. But not, Macklin decided, if A was expecting that. Sometimes a simple line of work could make Form 1040 read like a child's primer.

The feds were easier. Tonight they had exchanged the diaper service van for another with no advertising on it, a civilian vehicle parked two cars down with a sunset painted on its rear window. They had set up in front of the house because the light from the streetlamps aided their cameras and because they were assigned to keep track of who went in and came out as guests, not who sneaked in uninvited. Macklin started the Nissan, pulled out and around the van, and cruised down the less adequately lit side street north of Maggiore's lot. There he parked and got out and let himself easily over the low wall surrounding the house and yard. The Colt's butt gouged him a little during the climb, but that was okay. It took his mind off the incipient pain crawling across his lower back.

Pontier found Sergeant Lovelady seated on the grass a little off from the gang of uniformed cops in short sleeves lining up barricades against no crowd at all. Belle Isle was no place to be late on a Saturday night, even in warm weather. When Lovelady spotted his superior approaching he got to his feet with that peculiar grace exhibited by fat men everywhere, brushing grass off his yellow sportcoat and straightening out the roll at the top of his trousers. Pontier was dressed more casually in a blue Windbreaker and jeans and running shoes.

"Sorry, Inspector," said the sergeant. "You said to get you when anything came up on this one."

"I meant it when I said it. Who found her?"

"Kid dipping for carp. Thought it was some kind of float and waded out and pulled it in to shore. He didn't cop the smell till then. Tossed his cookies over there on the beach."

"I'll take in that sight some other time. He here?"

"Sent him home. He was busting curfew as it was. I got his folks' number and a statement to go on." He patted his right hip pocket, bulging with a notepad and Sergeant Lovelady.

"How long in the water?"

"Maybe a week, from the smell. M.E.'s there now. My guess is she got tangled up in reeds or a rusty Model A with a stiff in it left over from Prohibition and just broke loose. Maybe got tipped into the water up around St. Clair Shores. Someone would of seen her before this if she drifted much further."

"Someone might've anyway. Let's have a look."

"Be ready for it," the sergeant warned.

The body had been placed on a coroner's black rubber bag that had been unzipped and spread flat on the ground sloping toward the water. Black, nude, and fat even before bloating, it lay spreadeagled like a monstrous parade balloon with belly and breasts distended, its features lost in puffs of dark dough. The remains of a modest Afro hennaed almost orange stuck out in clumps streaked green with algae. The corpse looked artificial in the harsh beam of the police strobes with the flat surface of Lake St. Clair stretching behind it and the lights of Detroit spangling the mainland beyond. The stench was a living creature writhing in the still air. Not a few of the uniformed officers present were smoking. The tobacco acted as a disinfectant.

The medical examiner was a young woman with large-framed eyeglasses and sandy hair cropped close at the temples and nape and tumbling in a sort of carnation over her forehead. She had on sandals and corduroy slacks and a man's gray workshirt with the tail hanging out over the slacks. She had put away her instruments in a black metal box and was standing with one foot propped up on it, smoking a cigarette. Lovelady introduced her as Dr. Langan.

"There's a hole at the base of the skull that might have been made by a small-caliber bullet," she said without preamble. "If so it passed through the spot where the spinal cord meets the brain."

"The medulla oblongata," Pontier said.

She started a little. "Yes. Well, I may find any number of other causes when I get inside, but that hole was more than enough to induce brain death if it's as deep as it looks. Whether her lungs were still working when she went in depends on how much water I find in them."

"Show him what else you found," said Lovelady.

From her shirt pocket she drew a tiny glittering something on the end of a gold chain and handed it to Pontier, who examined the crucifix. "I had to pry it out of a crease in her neck," she said. "That must be how the killer missed it when he stripped the body."

Lovelady said, "It's the same kind worn by the sisters in Sunsmith's choir. It's why I called you."

Weighing the ornament and chain in his palm, the inspector looked down at the body. "Pleased to make your acquaintance, Sister Vernal."

"Think Sister Lucinda did her?" asked Lovelady.

"I don't know. She used a .38 on Sunsmith."

Dr. Langan said, "I just guessed a bullet. Hole like that, could have been an awl or an icepick."

"Thanks, Doc. Okay to call you Doc?"

"Just don't call me honey."

The detectives walked away from the stench.

"Icepick, shit, where do they get them?" Lovelady said. "I ain't seen one in a hardware store since I bet I was twelve."

Pontier thrust the crucifix at him for bagging. "Even less likely if it was Caroline Vetters. She wasn't a stone killer, just someone they hopped up and pointed in the Reverend's direction. We'll do a sweep. Pull the file on every mechanic we got and ask them some questions."

"What, Detroit?"

"Detroit, Birmingham, Southfield, downriver, the Pointes—hell, call Iroquois Heights, use our markers. If it walks and it kills for money I want to talk to it."

"Jesus. I retire in two months."

"Smartasses retire quicker than that, Sergeant."

"I hear you," Lovelady said.

The alarm system was nothing. They never were. Macklin shorted it out with a penny, jimmied open the french doors leading in from the pool, and stood inside the anteroom to the library letting his eyes adjust themselves to the darkness indoors. Not even a deadbolt lock. It was surprising how much faith even someone as cautious as Charles Maggiore placed in walls and an exclusive location.

After two minutes he began moving, feeling his way with his feet for any new furniture that might have been added since he had last visited the house as a guest. For the rest, he had drawn his floor plan from a memory that he had spent years training. The Colt Shooting Master was in his right hand.

The library door was open. Maggiore wasn't in that room. Macklin determined that much after five minutes of excruciating advancement. He was aware of the time, although he had removed his wristwatch to avoid catching moonlight on its face; the clock in his head—a natural convenience, not an acquired one—was accurate to within a few seconds. He timed his movements, sensing a trap.

Maggiore wasn't in the living room or in the kitchen or in the dining alcove. From that room, bulletproof bow windows looked out on Lake St. Clair a brisk swim north of the spot where Wayne County Morgue attendants were busy moving a body found beached on Belle Isle. The bedroom and bathroom were deserted. Macklin found the door leading down to the basement gym. It was where Maggiore spent half his life.

The room, illuminated grayly through two rectangular windows at ground level, was silent, smelling faintly of leather from the punching bag and exercise horse and of Sicilian sweat. The perspiration odor had an odd effect on Macklin. It represented his first personal contact in months with the man who had tried to have him killed while they were ostensibly working on the same team; the man who, failing that, had lured Macklin's son into the business of killing. A modern Mediterranean, the man nevertheless understood the power to be gained through the slow murder of the soul.

Macklin waited for the sensation to pass. He had always worked from an emotionless base; beyond professional pride it was of little moment to him who lived and who died or how. You did a thing enough times until you could do it without thinking, grooving in your muscles and reactions like a key worn to a certain lock. It was the way to success and the way away from guilt and madness. But the sensation did not pass, and time was growing short. Gordy would be finishing up his telephone conversation by now. He had ten minutes at most.

He had taken a step toward the only door in the room other than the entrance when it sprang open and darkness dissolved in a flash of red and yellow. But before the report imploded his eardrums, he aimed the Colt at the crooked figure outlined by the flash and put two into the left side of its chest. His own muzzle flare receded and into its place rushed noise and darkness and pain.

CHAPTER 9

The church where the Reverend Thomas Aquinas Sunsmith held forth twice Sundays and all day Christmas Day had started out Catholic, only to be placed on the market when the Vatican had decided to consolidate the archdiocese during the money crunch of the late seventies. There it had languished for five years, a steepled white elephant with no resale value except to another man of God, who bought it outright with his share of the proceeds from his group's one hit record. He had added more pews, placed amplifiers where the votive candles had stood, and turned the rectory into dressing rooms for the sisters and a big office for himself with a white shag rug, an altar-shaped desk topped with black onyx, and a portrait of himself in mauve robes done in Day-Glo on black velvet in a silver frame as big as a barn door. The walls were paneled in yellow oak and a mounted copy of the group's gold record occupied a spot level with a framed certificate of ordination.

Roger studied the latter while waiting for Sunsmith's

entrance. He was wearing a brown corduroy sportcoat over a clean pair of jeans and his only necktie, blue polyester with a pink stripe, and he had combed his hair and shaved. His gun was at home. Good thing, because before being allowed into the rectory he had been frisked expertly by the black police officer he had spotted on television earlier, while the Reverend's four huge bodyguards looked on. He hadn't seen Mercer, who was busy changing along with the other sisters for the late service, but one of the giants had his name in a notebook and after the search he had been conducted into the office and told to wait. The bodyguards all moved like men wearing guns. Church had changed since Roger's Sunday school days.

His inspection of the office had yielded nothing of use to him. The desk was bare on top, the drawers empty but for sermon notes and stationery and hundreds of guitar picks. The guitar itself, red and silver and shaped like a scimitar, leaned on its amplifier in a corner. If there was a safe it wasn't hidden in any of the standard places. There were no books, unless one counted six big Bibles on a shelf in assorted colors to match the Reverend's robes. Four shelves running the length of the east wall contained dated videotapes that Roger guessed were of the Sunday services. They were broadcast locally on cable and syndicated across the country. Roger shifted his attention from the ordination certificate to the glow-in-the-dark painting of the big brown man in mauve and wondered if he wore a bulletproof vest under his robes.

The man himself entered, bald head shining, square body sheathed in a royal-blue three-piece piped in gold like a band uniform, orange necktie held in place on a matching shirt by a big gold clasp in the shape of a musical clef. He showed Roger a grin as big as the room and crushed his hand and sat him in a chair upholstered in white leather and slid one hand onto the edge of the desk. He was even more physically overwhelming in person, with a face the size of a caricature's and heat radiating out from his center as from an ambulatory furnace. "Sister Mercer speaks highly of you," he rumbled. "I hope you two have been discreet."

"About this meeting? I didn't—"

"About your affair. Of course she thinks she's in love with you. I don't ask the sisters to be angels anywhere but in the choir, but I do require they display good judgment in how they conduct their personal lives. Well, you've come to talk about working in the service of the Lord."

"The service—"

"I'll start. Your name isn't Martin and everything you know about public relations you could poke through a buttonhole. Your name is Roger Macklin. You have a history of arrests in this area for possession of narcotics. You spent two months in a drug rehabilitation center in Farmington Hills last year. Your father's name is Peter Macklin, a hired killer for the Boniface family, or he was before he went independent. Young Mr. Macklin, I could have had the elders shoot you down when you showed up at the church and the case would never have gone to trial."

The elders were evidently what Sunsmith called his bodyguards. Consciously, Roger convinced himself he had accepted all this without moving a muscle in his face. Subconsciously he was aware that his mouth was open. He closed it, worked his tongue from side to side to gather lubrication, and said: "Who told you all that?"

"Christians have friends all over. Did you think because Sister Mercer recommended you you could just walk in here and pick your spot to shoot me?"

"Shoot you? No kidding, *shoot* you? You thought that?" Roger felt himself recovering. Sunsmith hadn't mentioned anything he couldn't have gotten off a police blotter. "Hell, why'd I want to shoot *you*?"

"One of the sisters tried to shoot me in this church one week ago. I hope you'll excuse me if I suspect a complete stranger of entertaining the same designs."

"Was any of those arrests for murder or attempted murder?"

"No, but then neither was any of Sister Lucinda's."

"Hey, I don't talk to my dad since I found out what he does. I don't even go deer hunting. Look, I fucked up my life with the drugs, but I'm off them now and I'm looking to start again, that's all."

Sunsmith showed all his teeth. "You found Christ in rehab, that it?"

"I might say it if I thought you were dumb enough to buy it. Guy in my ward, he saw Joseph when he was on meth. Said he knew it was Joseph on account of he had that worried look like you'd have if your wife told you it was God's baby she was having. Anyway, I hear the guy's in El Salvador now reading the New Testament to the *contras*. Me, I was to see a burning bush I'd figure some kids set it on fire smoking shit. I ain't been to church since I was little. I need a job is all. Something interesting enough to keep me from pumping my veins full of crap."

"That why you took up with Mercer?"

"No, that just happened. The job idea came after."

The big man sat swinging one leg, his large fingers drumming the desk in four-beat time. He said: "I don't ask everyone I hire to believe. One of the elders is a Muslim and I think Jesus turned the ancestor of my publicist out of the temple at Jerusalem. I ask merely that everyone does his work and does not slander this church."

"That mean I get a chance to show you what I can do?"

"Don't think I'm a fool because I dress like this." He slid off the desk to tower over Roger. "Jesus knew that one of the apostles would betray Him but took no steps to protect Himself. I am constructed along different lines. Go from this place, Mr. Martin-Macklin. If you return, I can't answer for the elders' actions. There is lamentably little of Jesus in their natures as well."

After leaving the rectory, Roger drove his old Duster

around a series of corners until he was sure nobody was following him, then popped for full service in a station on McNichols while he placed a call from the public telephone next to the men's room. It rang a couple of times before someone answered.

"It's me," said Roger. "I'm having trouble delivering the package."

The man on the other end paused. "Okay. We'll talk where we met last time. Two o'clock."

Roger said okay and hung up.

"What happens at two o'clock?"

Michael Boniface, looking his age behind a cobweb-gray overnight stubble with his belly hanging over the tie of his robe, shuffled in from his bedroom in a stiff new pair of leather slippers. His feet had grown accustomed to the disposable green sponge-rubber items issued to the inmates at Milan. The golden retriever got up from the carpet and trotted over to have its ears scratched.

"Nothing." Picante replaced the receiver. He was fully dressed in his shabby suit and skinny out-of-date necktie. "I was just ordering breakfast."

"Didn't I hear the phone ring?"

"No."

"Shit. I thought it might be Macklin."

Picante looked at him quickly, hesitated. "Oh. No, it wasn't him."

"They don't serve breakfast before two o'clock?" Boniface pushed the dog away. "Hell, the service was better at Milan."

"Two o'clock's when they stop serving it."

"Good. I'm hungry enough to eat the mutt."

Picante uncased his long teeth in a grin.

CHAPTER 10

Gordy thought it would be like in the movies.

In the movies, the emergency room was right outside surgery so the people who were waiting to find out what happened inside could come rushing up when the doctor pushed through the swinging doors in his greens with the mask dangling and gave them the news. It was always that way and you saw it so many times you never questioned it and couldn't picture it any other way.

At Detroit Receiving Hospital, the nurse behind the desk that looked like a cigarette counter in a hotel hung up the telephone and summoned Gordy over and told him Dr. Stepp would see him in his office. She might have been a receptionist informing him the personnel manager was ready to interview him.

The office was half a mile down a quiet corridor and one floor up via an elevator that made no noise at all. The place reminded him of the set of a futuristic movie from the fifties.

He wondered if other people thought so much in terms of Hollywood when they visited a hospital.

There he found himself in the presence of a red-headed eighteen-year-old kid in a camel's-hair sportcoat and red silk tie, who placed in his care a hand so pink and well scrubbed it might have belonged to a mannequin and asked him to sit down. He declined. The kid didn't sit either and put his hands in his pockets.

"Your friend is in Intensive Care," he said. "I don't want to operate just yet. He was about a quart low on blood when we got him." It sounded accusatory.

"He was laying in the basement when I found him. I don't know for how long. I was only gone fifteen minutes or so. I took him straight here, didn't want to wait around for an ambulance."

"You were wise not to. Nine-eleven is a joke in this town. We pumped two units back into him and we're waiting for his condition to stabilize before we go in after those bullets. Did the nurse tell you what saved him?"

"The nurse told me shit."

"It's a hell of a thing," said Dr. Stepp, placing a hand on the back of his neck; and from his language Gordy felt that some kind of barrier had been broken through. The bodyguard figured he was older than eighteen after all. "Do you know anything about your friend's medical history? His birth?"

"I just work for him."

"Well, it's just a theory. Birth defects are sort of a hobby with me. I was thinking of specializing in that area when thoracics caught my fancy. The X-rays showed some things in the epidermal hump on his left shoulder that shouldn't be, a partially developed ribcage and a bit of lumbar vertebrae. Yet he has a full set of his own. It's my thought he's wearing part of his unborn twin."

"Jesus."

"It's not really all that uncommon. Some years ago, doctors in South Africa operating on what they thought was an abdominal ulcer found a withered fetus in a thirty-year-old man's large intestine. He'd carried around his sister all that time without suspecting."

"So how'd that save Mr. Maggiore?"

"Well, in the case of mirror-image twins, only one has the standard equipment in the standard places. The other will have his heart, liver, appendix, and pancreas on the opposite side."

"Jesus."

"The nurse who prepped him couldn't figure out why he was still breathing when she saw those holes on the left side of his chest. The X-rays provided the answer." Stepp smiled. "I don't know what kind of terms you're on with your boss, but if we get lucky and pull him through this you might tell him he made it this far because his heart *isn't* in the right place."

Gordy couldn't picture himself saying that to Mr. Maggiore. "Can I see him?"

"I'd rather no one but the staff saw him until after the operation."

"I'll stand out of traffic. Nobody'll know I'm there."

Stepp's eyes flicked up and down Gordy's massive length, but he made no response to the statement. "Your boss is safe. The police have men stationed outside ICU. Incidentally, one of them wants to talk to you, an Inspector Pontier. He's in the other waiting room."

"Take good care of Mr. Maggiore, Doc."

"I mean to. There's a paper in this."

The big man went through the door indicated. The bald black detective who had come to see his employer a few days earlier was seated on a sherbet-green sofa with his legs crossed, turning the pages in a copy of the *National Geographic*.

"Reading about this guy who found the Spanish galleon off Key West," he said, without glancing up. "Four hundred million in gold and silver. He lost a son and a daughter-in-law looking for it but he says it was worth it. What do you think of that?"

"Depends on the son and daughter-in-law." Gordy stood over the detective with his hands folded in front of him.

"Maggiore's in good hands. Any doctor who keeps the *National Geographic* in his waiting room is all right. Stay away from the ones with *People* and *Reader's Digest*." He laid the magazine on an orange coffee table and looked up. "Do your legs bend?"

"I sat in the car coming over."

"Give my neck a break and do it again."

After a second the bodyguard stepped in front of a chair upholstered in salmon-colored vinyl and let himself down on it, sitting stiffly on the edge of the cushion with his hands resting on his knees. The room's walls were pastel blue and a watercolor done after Toulouse-Lautrec hung opposite the window. The place looked like the inside of a freezer at Baskin-Robbins.

"Who did Maggiore?" Pontier asked.

"I don't know."

"Come on."

"I found him laying in his blood in the gym in the basement."

"That's for the report. I want to know who you figure did it."

"I don't know."

Pontier uncrossed his legs, recrossed them in the other direction. "I pulled your file. You don't have one. You're not one of these Fifth Amendment lugs. You're not even Italian. That *omerta* crap fits you like a tent. We don't pick up this shooter, a gang war gets started, your job as bodyguard gets harder."

"I don't know means I don't know."

"Let's review this past week." The inspector tapped his knee. "Last Sunday. One of the sisters in the Reverend

Sunsmith's choir tries to whack him and gets whacked by Sunsmith's defensive line. Monday. Michael Boniface gets sprung from Milan and almost gets whacked in Belleville. Saturday night. The body of the sister who was supposed to be singing in place of the sister who tried to whack Sunsmith boogies ashore at Belle Isle. That same night someone tries to whack Maggiore, who as everyone knows is against Sunsmith on the casino gambling question and needs gambling legalized so he can hold the place that used to belong to Boniface. Aside from the fact that with all this attempted whacking going on the only person who gets whacked was the least important person in the whole mess, what have we learned?"

"We learned that you like the word *whack*."

Surprised, Pontier grinned behind his moustache. "That's pretty good. I never met one of you trained sides of beef with a sense of humor before. No, what we learned is something is getting set to blow. Being a peace officer, I'm naturally concerned in seeing that it doesn't, whatever it is, and that's where you can help."

"Wish I could."

"That's your answer?"

Before Gordy could reply, a door opened in from the corridor and a fat man stuffed into a yellow sportcoat entered and bent over Pontier, murmuring in a tone too low for the bodyguard to pick out words. The inspector listened without taking his eyes off Gordy.

"Who's spelling him?" he asked.

"Sergeant Twill," murmured the fat man.

"Ledyard's here?"

"On the phone at the nurses' desk."

" 'Kay." Pontier stood. He was several inches taller than the fat man, but probably weighed far less. "Book this son of a bitch. Take his gun."

The fat man looked at Gordy with eyes no deeper than the dimples in his pocked face. "Material witness?"

"Suspicion of attempted murder." To Gordy: "Stupid smart men are the worst. The Wayne County Jail's full of them." He left while the fat man was standing the bodyguard up for the frisk.

"Did not Satan inveigle God Himself into wagering the fate of Job, His good and loyal servant? And was not this an evil act?"

Pontier turned down the portable radio on his desk. Even with the volume almost off, the Reverend's baritone set the transistors buzzing. He watched Lovelady coming in. It was a warm Sunday for spring and the sergeant had peeled off his sportcoat and sweated through his shirt.

"Sunsmith's on a roll this morning," Pontier said. "You run King Kong down to County?"

"I put him in holding. Thought you'd want to talk to him some more."

"I'd rather try cracking glass with a hard look. We'll hang on to him tonight and spring him in the morning. He got my goat is all. How much did Ledyard tell you over the phone?"

"Just what I told you. Something about Sunsmith."

"Ledyard's been cooling leather in interesting places since he started babysitting the Reverend. Philip Constable's office. Carmen Thalberg's place in Bloomfield Hills."

"Constable." Lovelady's slab of a face creased in thought. "President of Disiran Chemicals?"

"Yeah. Mob front."

"Not really, but Charles Maggiore's a heavy investor. Constable was a Boniface consig before Maggiore took over and handed him Disiran. Some other names and companies to check out, and Carmen Thalberg. How's that for a couple, the evangelist and the stinking-rich widow?"

"Maybe they got a thing. It's a hell of a strange world."

"Maybe not that strange. I want to talk to her, Constable too. And run this list through the computer and see what it kicks out." He slid a handwritten sheet across the desk.

"How's chances of nailing down Disiran's investments over the past year?"

"Like I said, I retire in two months."

The inspector turned the radio all the way off. The sisters were singing "Bless'd Be the Lessons of the Lamb." "Maggiore's under hack with the IRS, right?"

"When a mob guy's up on one charge it's practically automatic."

"We got any fed friends?"

"Randall Burlingame, if you want to call him a friend. But he's on retirement leave."

"Ring him up, see can he deal us a copy of Maggiore's tax records. How's the sweep coming?"

"Still sweeping. Couple of dopers in holding ought to start splitting open any time now. But the hit on Sister Vernal had too much class for them."

"Brief me when you get someone worth leaning on. And let me know what you shake down on this other stuff. You going to be able to remember all this shit?"

Lovelady folded the handwritten list and poked it into his shirt pocket. "Remembering shit is my life."

The bleeding had stopped finally.

Macklin had been moving as soon as the door sprang open in Maggiore's basement, and as he returned fire had barked his left elbow hard on the steel shaft of a Nautilus resistance machine in the center of the room, knocking off a piece of flesh and numbing the bone all the way down to the wrist. His victim was still falling when Macklin heard tires swishing on the asphalt driveway. He had stumbled up the stairs, cradling his elbow with the hand still holding the gun, ducked as a headlight shaft raked the windows on the ground floor, and let himself out the french doors at poolside just as the motor was dying. Before climbing back over the wall he had pitched the gun into the pool. Police technicians could treat it until doomsday and never trace it back further than the body in the basement.

By the time he had abandoned the stolen Nissan he had bled through his shirt and sportcoat and stained the front seat. He had wiped off everything he had touched and then tied the handkerchief around his arm at the elbow for the eleven-block walk back to his house. There he had stripped, cleaned the three-cornered tear with alcohol, bandaged the arm, and slept the rest of the night, half-waking from time to time with the throbbing. When he awoke in morning light the wound had stopped bleeding, but it hurt him to bend the arm.

He showered, shaved, exchanged the crusty bandage for a smaller one, dressed in a sportshirt and slacks, and went out to the curb carrying the bundle of ruined clothing, which he mixed in with the other trash awaiting collection. By that time he was ravenous. He had eaten nothing since breakfast the morning before.

The radio in the kitchen played low while he measured coffee into an urn left behind by his ex-wife and draped four strips of bacon sizzling into the frying pan on the stove. When the news came on he turned up the volume.

"The President prepares for the Pope's visit to Washington," intoned the announcer. "FDA orders cans of contaminated mushrooms removed from supermarket shelves in three states. Two men missing and believed dead when their single-engine plane disappears over Lake Michigan. And locally, an alleged mob kingpin is in critical condition following an attempt on his life last night. Those are the headlines; details following these messages."

"Christ." Macklin burned his finger on the pan and slid it off the gas flame to keep the sizzling from drowning out the radio. Sucking the finger, he waited for details. Even in the dim receding light of the muzzle flashes he had seen the stains spreading on Maggiore's light-colored blazer high up on the left side. He wondered if the announcer was speaking from new information or if he was still going on an early report from the hospital.

The announcer was still talking about contaminated mushrooms when the doorbell rang. Cursing again, Macklin left the kitchen, crossed through the living room, and put his eye to the peephole in the front door. Two big black men in moustaches and long sideburns stood on his small front porch, wearing the brown-trimmed dark blue uniforms issued by the Detroit Police Department.

CHAPTER 11

Picante ate with one forearm resting on the table across his chest and used his fingers to push carrots and peas onto his fork. When his mouth was full he washed down the contents with a slug of Dago red. He called it that, explaining that he was four generations removed from the old country and that all the Italian he knew you could get off the outside of a box of Mueller's spaghetti. Roger, no fashion plate himself, looked at Picante's suit and wondered if it was the only one he had ever owned. There was a fresh gravy stain on his skinny tie.

"Anyway," Picante said, scooping a big forkful of whipped potatoes into his mouth, further jeopardizing the tie, "I left the guy's head in this big basket of fruit on the doorstep for his missus to find when she got home from work. Wish I could of stuck around and seen the look on her face."

Roger pushed aside his chef's salad half finished and lit a cigarette. His appetite came and went by turns, and his companion's stories weren't helping. "What if somebody else found it first?"

"Hell, I never thought of that." He chewed with his mouth open, considering it. "Well, hell, the effect is the same, right? I mean, a head in a fruit basket, who'd think of it? I had style, not like your old man. He's about the best around, don't get me wrong. He just ain't got no imagination."

"I wasn't going to stick up for him. We don't get on."

"That's too bad. You could learn from him. I had to make all my own mistakes. I made my bones with this little .25 Browning I bought off a junkman in Sandusky. Chased the guy for four blocks with two in his belly before I got him in this blind alley—"

The waiter, a reedy young blond man, came around asking with a lilt in his voice if everything was all right. "Fine," Picante said abruptly. "Just great." When the waiter left, he leaned forward and lowered his voice. "I jammed the piece in his mouth and fired, and would you believe he spit the bullet out at me? Didn't even penetrate the roof of his mouth. So I put one in each eye and that did it finally. I didn't know then that a .22 has more power than a .25, can you believe anybody ever being that dumb?"

"What'd you do with the head?"

"Well, by then there wasn't time—" He broke off and sat back, picking up his wine glass. "Think you're better than me, don't you? Just like your old man. Okay, I liked the work. We're still the same, you and me and Mighty Macklin. Cleaning up where the rich folks shit."

"You got out of it, though. I don't plan to make it my life's work either."

"That's where you're smarter than your old man. After thirty-five the pace gets to you. You start living to work instead of working to live, studying up, exercising, trying to put back what you lost getting older. Sooner or later it's all got to catch up."

Roger tapped some ash into the tin tray on the table. "I

don't know if I can get close enough to do Sunsmith now. That was a mistake, trying to hire on. I didn't figure him to make me so early."

"See, that's where some advice would of helped. Think he's pegged you?"

"He isn't sure. All he's got to go on is my sheet and that's just dope. But if his bodyguards make me inside of range they'll blow me down and cry over me later. I sure won't be able to get in, do him and get out again."

"You passing?"

"Not if you've got any ideas. I need the cash and the hit will look good on my résumé."

Picante drained his glass and signaled the waiter for a refill. He raised his eyebrows at Roger, who shook his head and pointed at his water glass. He was working on his vices. With that thought, he crushed out the cigarette and didn't light another.

After the waiter had gone: "Let me work on it. I'm not in a position to just unplug one shooter and plug in another. You're still living in the same place?"

Roger nodded. "I got to ask a question."

"Why Sunsmith?"

"Right. I mean, your boss doesn't want to see gambling made legal on account of that'd firm up Maggiore, and Maggiore's job is what he's after. Knock down Sunsmith and there's no one to stand in the way of the casinos."

"You think it's that easy, how come Maggiore hasn't knocked him down before this? That fight's been going on for months."

"Well, he's been busy with those gunrunning charges and all."

"Uh-uh. He clears the way for casino gambling, he gets all the backing he needs to blow the feds' case out of the water. Sunsmith dead is the last thing he wants. That's the mistake the Romans made with Christ. They should of bought him off. Only Maggiore tried that and Sunsmith just took the money and kept on. He gets dead, gambling goes down big so he didn't die in vain."

"I think I'm getting it," said Roger after a minute. "It makes my head hurt."

Picante grinned, showing his long teeth with a pea crushed between two of them. "The old double backspin. Just because I settled down don't mean I stopped putting heads in fruit baskets."

"So why hire me? I mean, Boniface's on good terms with my dad, isn't he?"

"Let's just say prison mellowed Mike." Picante drank Dago red. "He don't know what's good for him no more."

CHAPTER 12

The officer who came for Carmen was young and not bad-looking, with blond hair in need of trimming and a ginger moustache that was like a transparency on his bland face. If he shaved it off, no one would notice until he pointed it out. He had made a suit out of a blue navy blazer with brass buttons with anchors on them and a pair of blue wool trousers and he drove an unmarked gray Chrysler without chrome. On their way down Woodward Carmen noticed other cars slowing down as they drew near. They wouldn't have been much more obvious in a blue-and-white.

At 1300 Beaubien she was escorted to an office partitioned off behind amber pebbled glass, where an older fat man in a yellow sportcoat asked her to sit down and offered her coffee in a Styrofoam cup, which she accepted. Then he excused himself and left her alone to drink it. The walls were tacked all over with typewritten sheets and the metal desk was a jumble of manila file folders holding up a plastic coffee mug whose angle suggested it was stuck fast to the folder on top.

A framed photograph of an attractive black woman in her forties occupied the only clear corner of desk. Carmen could hear conversation buzzing in the squad room over the top of the partition.

After a few minutes she was joined by a tall bald black man with a moustache that would certainly make a difference if he shaved it off, who introduced himself as Inspector George Pontier and sat down behind the desk. He extracted the mug with a little tearing sound of paper, put it away in a drawer, and rearranged the clutter to give him an unobstructed view of his guest. He had gray eyes.

"It was kind of you to come down," he said. "I'd have been glad to talk to you in your home."

"I prefer visiting to being visited. This way I can get up and leave when I feel like it. It was kind of you to send someone," she added, softening the effect.

"Did the officer tell you what it was about?"

"Just my relationship with the Reverend Sunsmith. Is he all right? There hasn't been another attempt on his life." Her tone didn't change.

"No, he delivered two sermons this morning without interruption. The taxpayers will get the bill for that. The Russian ambassador had less security when he came through touring the auto plants."

"Good. I'm glad."

Pontier watched her. High cheekbones, good copper coloring going gold, no blusher, dark eyes contrasted against the tawny fall of hair to her shoulders. The cream blouse she was wearing was right for her and a thin gold necklace lay on her collarbone. She looked thirty but he knew she was older than that. "What is your relationship with the Reverend?"

"He's a friend. Also I donate to his church."

"May I ask why?"

"I'm a religious woman. I come from a religious country. And I believe in what he's doing."

"His faith is a far cry from Roman Catholicism."

"I left the Church when the current Pope ascended. It was hard to see God with him standing in the way."

That part sounded genuine enough. He thought he was beginning to read her, but he wasn't sure. "May I ask how long you've been associated with Sunsmith and how much you've donated?"

"I don't see why not. I record it when I make out my taxes. I attended one of his services for the first time about six months ago. I made a small donation then and I've been contributing ever since. It's up around a quarter million now. I'm sorry I don't have the exact figures with me, but you didn't say what you wanted when you called."

"That's a lot of money."

"I have a lot more."

"What is it about the Reverend that inspires your faith?"

"He believes in what he's saying."

"That's the reason?"

She changed positions. She had on tan poplin slacks that gave up a view of her slim ankles and bare feet in gold sandals when she crossed her legs. "Where I come from the Church is just another branch of the government. The padres are tools of the state to be used or discarded depending on their power to manipulate the people. Some of them here are no better. Not the Reverend. Oh, I know, he dresses like a clown and he loves to show off. But when the fire is on him it consumes him and everyone near him. It isn't an act. Why are you asking me these questions? Does it have something to do with the people who are trying to kill him?"

He touched his moustache. "Are you opposed to legalized gambling in the city of Detroit?"

"Yes."

"Some people, the mayor included, welcome the idea. They think it will create jobs, bring in revenue."

"The classified section is full of jobs if anyone wants one badly enough," she said. "I'm not just saying that because I have money now. My father was a poor man, and he wasn't too proud to do anything honest that would feed and clothe his family."

"Excuse me, but we're discussing Sunsmith, not your father."

"I'm not finished. Gambling is legal in my country. It brought in *las turistas, mucho dinero*. My father tried to get a job working for the casinos—busboy, bellhop, anything. They laughed at him when he applied, the *norteamericanos* who owned the gambling business. They said the Americans who came down there to spend money didn't want to be bothered by a lot of little brown greasers jabbering at them in pidgin English. If they wanted that they'd hire a bus and tour the villages. All of the employees came down from the north with the equipment, they said, and then they threw my father out into the street."

She caught herself snapping her consonants and relaxed. Pontier watched the elegant foreign-born widow creep back in. "It would be the same here," she said. "Ask Atlantic City how many new jobs there are there now, them with their crooked little maze of holding corporations leading back to the underworld and double the crime rate they had before the casinos came. I'll put my faith in the Reverend's pink robes."

The inspector smiled at the picture of his wife on the desk. Do you believe this? Aloud he said, "I don't think you contribute to Sunsmith's church because you like his sermons. I think you're investing in him like he's a business and he's turning it back in a cash profit under the table and off the books while you declare the principal as a legitimate tax deduction. That's what I think."

"Inspector, I have millions. I pay more to lawyers to keep down my taxes than you pay in taxes. Why would I want to become involved in anything as complex as that?"

She didn't get indignant or make her eyes round and protest her innocence. He gave her that much.

"Because the more money you have the more you want, and especially when you come from a country where the government owns everything and you don't want this one to own anything more than you figure it has coming," he said. "Because avoiding taxes is as American as Elvis. You're not the first one of Sunsmith's suckers I've talked to this morning, Mrs. Thalberg. I know the scam." Which was untrue. Lovelady hadn't been able to locate Philip Constable yet and he was still tracking down the others on the list.

"Suckers?"

"The Reverend doesn't pull in that much, not enough to satisfy as many businesses and individuals as he's connected with and the amount of money they have to invest. Excuse me, donate. He's siphoning off cash from the later donors to satisfy the original donors at the top of the pyramid. Which is good for them but not so good for the latecomers at the bottom. When it all caves in, as it has to sooner or later, they're the ones who will get squashed the worst. Where do you figure in there, Mrs. Thalberg?"

She flicked something off the crease of her slacks with a buffed nail. "You're building an impressive pyramid of your own," she said. "Guesses on top of guesses. This sounds more like a case for Fraud, not Homicide."

"I don't care who he's screwing out of their money. I couldn't care less if you paid your taxes in dollars or toothpicks or not at all. It's no skin off my nose if gambling passes or it doesn't, although if it does I'll just be dealing with a different class of scroat. But I'm no financial genius, and if I've figured out Sunsmith's game by what little I have to go on, someone else must have too. If that someone else is the sort that would hire a killer to balance his books, *then* I care. I'm paid to."

"You suspect me?"

"If you can show me a reason why I shouldn't, it would make my job a lot easier."

"Am I under arrest?"

He shook his head without taking his eyes off her. She smirked.

"Because I look innocent?"

"Because I think that if you wanted to kill someone you'd do it yourself." He rose. "I'm just pulling in all the checkers, seeing if one of them wants to jump on any of the others. Thanks again for coming down, Mrs. Thalberg."

After a second she stood. "You have an odd style, Inspector."

"The deputy chief thinks so, too. Sergeant Lovelady will see you get home."

She hadn't seen him move toward the intercom, but when she turned, the fat detective in the yellow coat was holding the door. She looked back.

"Is it just in the movies that the detective tells the suspect not to leave town?"

"Pretty much. But if you're planning any long trips I'd appreciate your telling me where you can be reached."

She said she would.

On their way out, Carmen and Lovelady passed a man in early middle age being ushered into the squad room between two police officers in uniform. The man barely glanced at her with tired eyes and then the three went through another door that swung shut behind them. She would have thought nothing of it, except Sergeant Lovelady paused to watch the procession.

"Who was that?" she asked.

"Peter Macklin." It came out automatically. Then, as an afterthought, he placed his shoulder between her and the door through which the trio had gone and put a hand on her elbow, steering her toward the corridor.

"Who did he kill?"

The fat man looked at her blankly.

"It was a joke," she said.

He escorted her out.

CHAPTER 13

An hour after the late service on Sunday morning, Sister Mercer tried to hang herself from the light fixture in her bathroom, but the generally poor construction of the apartment building saved her when the fixture came loose along with four square feet of plaster and she fell to the floor, striking her head on the base of the toilet. Sister Asaul, whom the Reverend had sent to stay with her, was in the kitchen drinking coffee at the time and investigated the noise and called the Reverend and an ambulance, in that order.

Sunsmith beat the paramedics to the scene in a red velour jogging suit that he had bought at the beginning of his new fitness campaign and stayed with Mercer, holding her hand and murmuring soothing phrases, while Asaul kept damp the cloth on her forehead. The four elders and Sergeant Twill, who was spelling Paul Ledyard that Sunday, let the attendants and a uniformed officer through and the officer wrote down in his pad that Sister Mercer had slipped on a wet spot on the bathroom floor. Asaul and the Reverend had agreed on that point before she dialed 911. After that he followed the ambulance to Detroit Receiving in his limousine.

In the waiting room outside Emergency, being stared at by others sitting vigil on loved ones consigned to the facility's aspirin-bottle interior, Sunsmith decided he needed more cash. The referendum to place casino gambling on the November ballot was just three weeks and two days away, and in his desk at the rectory were the results of a private poll that stated more than thirty percent of the voters in Detroit were undecided as to how they would vote on the measure. In three weeks the attempt on his life would be forgotten along with all its publicity dividends, and he was too big a target to risk inviting another. When Asaul had called with the news about Mercer he had thought for a split second about turning her suicide attempt to political advantage, then decided that the whole thing about Roger Macklin was too indistinct to serve him much good, and anyway, female members of a holy man's entourage who tried to hang themselves raised unhealthy speculation in the jaded minds of the public.

He needed open-air rallies and commercial spots on radio and television and full-page ads and prime-time telethons to hammer home the abysmal sin of government-sanctioned gambling. Such things were expensive, and as long as he had to keep funneling new investments back to the original investors, the upkeep on the church and his own Sunday morning cablecast would continue to eat up the difference. Taking on new investors only compounded the problem, and yet he had to do that in order to satisfy the later investors when they grew impatient waiting for returns on funds already in the hands of their predecessors. It was like turning the handle of a winch attached to a golden chain that got heavier and harder to pull with each turn, but that if he let go of it would whirl around and take off his head on the backlash. What he had to do was propose something that would loosen the current investors' pocketbooks, something sweet enough to overcome all their doubts and suspicions and sweep away the gambling threat on a tide of paper currency.

At the end of an hour an emergency nurse came out to inform Sunsmith that Sister Mercer appeared to be out of danger, but that the doctor wanted to admit her overnight for observation in case of a concussion. The Reverend agreed distractedly. By then he had begun putting together his plan to run for the United States Congress.

On Monday morning, Pontier found Randall "Red" Burlingame, Michigan regional director of the Federal Bureau of Investigation, tuning up his blue Ford Escort with a Sears kit in the driveway of his brick ranch-style in suburban Farmington. The square, graying redhead looked older and softer in old green workpants and a white sweatshirt grown ratty at the ends of the sleeves, and when he bent over the engine to secure the wing nut on top of the air filter, Pontier saw that he was balding at the crown. At length Burlingame straightened, wiped off his hands on the last clean spot on a gray rag crumpled on top of the radiator, and got in on the driver's side to start the engine. It took off immediately and ran smoothly until he cut the ignition.

"Fuck certified mechanics," he said, climbing out. "Excuse my French. Garage wanted to soak me fifteen bucks for what I just did in five minutes."

"That IRS report," Pontier reminded him.

"Inside." Burlingame slammed shut the door and the hood, stuffed the greasy rag into a hip pocket, and led the way into the house through the side door in the cluttered garage. In the kitchen, he took a can of Budweiser out of the refrigerator and offered it to Pontier, who declined. It was ten A.M.

The FBI man shrugged and popped the top. "Grace took our granddaughter shopping. She starts school in the fall."

"I didn't know you had a grandchild that old."

"She isn't. Grace is the one going to school." He drank. "She's forty-nine and she wants to learn how to type and take dictation. I'd be worried she was planning to divorce me, except with her fat thumbs she'll never graduate."

They passed through a small dining area and down two steps into a living room done in cool colors with a sliding glass door opening onto a backyard secluded from the neighbors by a bank of Scotch pines. Burlingame sat his guest in a green vinyl La-Z-Boy and went through another door, to return a moment later carrying his beer and a thick gray cardboard folder secured with a wide rubber band. He dropped it into the inspector's lap.

"I had to sign for it, so don't leave it at the laundromat," he said, half-reclining on a sofa that matched the chair. "The agent who swung it for me figured I have less to lose, being on retirement leave. But I got a pension to consider."

"I haven't lost a piece of evidence or rolled over on a source yet." Pontier removed the rubber band and flipped through the contents. "Thanks for the boost."

"Forget it. Anything that'll sink the hook deeper into Charles Maggiore just tickles me plumb to death."

"I hope your replacement has the same attitude."

"That's up to you. If they ring in some quiz kid from D.C. like I expect, you'll have the chance to bring him along, give him the benefit of your long experience in the interest of harmony in law enforcement. But if it's an old fart waiting out his thirty it'll be like pulling nails with your toes just to get him to run fingerprints for you."

The file information was all gibberish to Pontier at this point. He put the rubber band back on and drummed his fingers on the folder. "How do you like it so far? Retirement."

Burlingame shifted positions to pull the stained rag out of his hip pocket and waved it like a flag of truce. "That's my last gray suit. Day I left I had Grace turn them all into wipers.

All except one for burying friends and to be buried in myself." He flung the scrap of cloth onto the coffee table. "My old man worked his ass off his whole life so his kid wouldn't have to wear old clothes. I worked mine off my whole life so I could. Life's a joke."

Neither said anything for a moment. Pontier put his hands on the arms of the chair. "Well, thanks again."

"What do you figure to find that the IRS didn't?"

He subsided. "If I'm right, Maggiore's been declaring donations to the Reverend Sunsmith's church through one of his legitimate holding companies."

"That charlatan? What's the wop doing, buying indulgences?"

"I think it's a scam, and I think it goes both ways. If so, it makes a better motive for taking out the Reverend than his stand on gambling."

"Seems like a lot of homework wasted if Maggiore kicks off."

"I called the hospital this morning. His condition is stable. They're planning on operating to remove those slugs tomorrow. Then again it might not be Maggiore's signature on the contract. There are others involved."

"You do a sweep?"

"Doing it now."

"Anybody I know?"

"Well, Peter Macklin."

Burlingame grinned, not pleasantly. "The only work Macklin would do for Maggiore is drag his dead carcass out of the way of the door."

"We reeled him in on the hit on the choir singer. We're holding him on the try on Maggiore. If we get those slugs before Macklin gets sprung we might start building a case."

"I don't know what kind. Knowing Macklin, the gun's a mile downriver by now."

"All the bases get touched, anyway." Pontier stroked the edge of the folder with his thumb absently. "In an ideal world, Maggiore and Macklin would be pulling life for murder and the fags in Milan would be buggering Sunsmith's fat ass for the next ten years on income tax fraud."

The FBI man plucked a two-inch cigar stub out of the ashtray on the coffee table and appeared to be considering lighting it. "Yeah, but in an ideal world we'd both be in some other line of work."

"I could work on the line at Ford's."

"Like hell." He dropped the stub back into the tray and picked up his beer. "And neither could I."

A young man in a blue pinstripe suit with a bandage on his forehead who introduced himself as an attorney with Howard Klegg habeased Macklin out of Interrogation Monday evening. The killer signed for his valuables and accepted the lawyer's invitation of a ride home. He felt sticky under his clothes and he needed a shave. They were getting into the car parked in the blue zone in front of police headquarters when a gray Maserati pulled abreast and a dark-skinned woman with tawny hair rolled down the window on the passenger's side. "Lift, Mr. Macklin?"

She removed her yellow Polaroids, and Macklin recognized her from the squad room the previous day. She wasn't a cop, not driving a car like that. He glanced at the lawyer. "Thanks."

The young man measured out an inch of smile across the roof of his own car. "Good choice." He got in behind the wheel.

When Macklin was sitting beside her, the woman looked at him. "Aren't you going to buckle up?"

"I just got out of jail."

"Against the law."

He met her gaze until it faltered. "Right," she said, and shifted into low. They took off with a squeak of rubber.

Driving along Beaubien, she asked: "Where to, your place in Southfield?"

"I knew it," he said.

"Knew what?"

"Good-looking woman picks me up in front of thirteen hundred, it isn't because she was driving by and liked my posture."

"I looked you up. I was surprised you're listed."

"Where'd you go first, the Yellow Pages under Killers?"

"You do too have a sense of humor," she said. "I was told you didn't."

"I don't have much use for one in my work."

"You're pretty open about it."

"I just came off twenty-four hours in lockup. If there's anyone who doesn't know what I do, I haven't seen them since yesterday. Who are you?"

"Carmen Contrale Thalberg. I called the jail and they said you were in Holding at Police Headquarters. The officer I spoke to there told me you were being processed out. I just caught you."

They took the John Lodge north. She drove the Maserati like she was mad at it, making racing changes between lanes and seldom touching the brake. She had on a powder-blue blouse and a beige skirt, and when they passed under a light, Macklin saw that she was in her stockinged feet. A pair of silver high-heeled sandals rested on the console.

"I saw you when you were brought in yesterday," she said. "A detective told me who you were."

He wondered if she was one of these bored rich wives who fantasized about making it with criminals. He had been pursued by a couple, and if they'd looked anything like this one he might not have run so hard. But she wasn't wearing a wedding ring. Her only jewelry was a tiny gold crucifix that winked in the cleft between her breasts when she worked the shift. He was starting to feel not so tired.

As if she'd been following his thoughts, she said: "The car was a gift from my late husband. I like its looks, but it has too much engine for me, also it's hard to shift in the city. Would you like to drive?"

"Anything beyond three speeds is beyond me."

"I thought all American men liked to show off behind the wheel."

"Shit," he said.

The fuzzbuster on the dash bleeped. She slowed down. "What is?"

"Your dumb spic act. I think if you didn't want the accent it wouldn't be there. Let's get to why you picked me up."

"Hokay, Joe. There's a cassette tape in the glove compartment."

He found the compartment finally and opened it. It contained a pair of deerskin driving gloves—it was the first time he had ever found gloves in a glove compartment—and three cassette tapes in plastic boxes. "Which one?"

"The one without a label. Put it in the slot."

He was still figuring out the dashboard when she took the tape from him and rammed it through a hinged flap under the radio with the heel of her hand.

" 'And Ahab spake unto Naboth,' " boomed a voice out of hidden speakers, " 'saying, Give me thy vineyard, that I may have it for a garden of herbs, because it is near unto my house; and I will give thee for it a better vineyard than it; or, if it seem good to thee, I will give thee the worth of it in money.' "

The speaker paused. Then: "What do you say, brothers and sisters? Did Naboth leap at this offer of ready cash? Did he hold out for a better offer? No, brothers and sisters. Nabob said, 'The Lord forbid it me!' "

The woman raised her voice above the rolling tones. "Do you know who that is?"

Macklin said he did. He had started feeling tired again.

She drove for another mile before asking the question.

"Can anybody hire you?"

CHAPTER 14

The shooter was a thirty-three-year-old Arkansan named Caudhill who had served with Special Forces in Cambodia and of late had been operating a stolen credit card racket for the Truzzi family in Toledo. The Ohio State Police had questioned him in connection with the turnpike slayings of two part-owners of a Cleveland adult theater chain and he was due in court next Thursday to answer charges of extortion and assault with intent to commit great bodily harm in an unrelated case. The clerk behind the desk in the Pontchartrain lobby barely looked at him when he asked for the number of Michael Boniface's suite. He was of middle height but stocky, with ginger hair that he blew into a shelf over his forehead and a drooping moustache, and the blue Windbreaker he had on over a black turtleneck and faded Levi's concealed a weight-lifter's build and an Ithaca pump shotgun in a special harness with no stock and the barrel cut back to the side.

Armed with the number, he walked past the elevator entrance, where a security man in uniform waited to ask passengers to show their keys before going up, to a bank of in-house telephones. The telephone in Boniface's suite rang twice before a man's voice came on the line.

"This is the hotel cashier," Caudhill said. "I'm just confirming your call to Auckland, New Zealand, before I enter it on your bill."

"New *Zea*land?" said the voice. "You got the wrong room, pal."

"Suite Seven-sixteen, Michael Boniface?"

"Shit. You sure it wasn't Oakland, Michigan, something like that?"

"The charge is eighty-seven-fifty."

"Well, no one here called New Zealand."

"I see. Could Mr. Boniface come down and discuss it?"

"What's to discuss? The call never happened."

"Well, if there's a problem with the telephone company we'll need a denial in writing."

"Shit. I'll be down in ten minutes."

"Are you Mr. Boniface?"

"He's sleeping. This is his associate, Mr. Picante."

"I'm sorry, but we need Mr. Boniface's signature. The suite is registered in his name."

"Can't it wait till morning?"

"I'm afraid not. I'm making out the books and we're expecting the auditor from the parent company in the morning. It will just take a few minutes. Otherwise I'll have to enter the charge."

"Shit."

"Pardon?"

"Give us twenty minutes." Click.

Caudhill hung up and took a seat in the lounging area with a view of the elevators. The shotgun nudged his ribs.

The name of the desk clerk from whom he had obtained the suite number was Leon. A former bell captain taking night classes at the University of Detroit, he was having an affair with a maid on the fourth floor who thought he looked a little like James Brown. His duties included delivering the cash receipts to the bank at the end of the day, and although few guests were paying in cash these days there were still several hundred dollars to dispose of by late afternoon. He had applied for a limited permit to carry a concealed weapon for his protection during trips to and from the bank, but he had been turned down, and so he had bought a nickel-plated Browning .25 semiautomatic pistol that he carried all the time in his hip pocket under his Pontchartrain blazer. He kept it loaded, but so far no one had attempted to rob him.

Caudhill was sharing the lounging area with a plain-clothes sergeant named Richard Weinacre, called Dick D'Bruiser by his fellow officers with the Detroit Police Department General Service Division for his resemblance to the big broken-nosed professional wrestler with a voice like a chainsaw. Ostensibly engrossed in a battered paperback copy of *The Winds of War* on the settee, he was actually present to witness a meeting between the director of a local car-theft ring and a man who had flown in from Los Angeles to buy him out. It was his day off, but the promotion list was coming out next week and he had been a sergeant for eight years. He could taste the arrest every time he moved his tongue around the inside of his mouth. He favored a Colt Cobra .38 Special that he wore in an alligator holster next to his right kidney.

The head of hotel security was out sick that week. In his place, a local firm had sent a former FBI field agent, one David W. Thornton, who had left the Bureau at age thirty-seven to marry the daughter of a Libyan oil millionaire who had then disinherited her. Forty now, with two children and one coming, he moonlighted days as a private detective. He was a good investigator with a sound federal man's idea of how to dress. His confidence was highest in well-tailored brown suits that complemented his wavy hair with the silver showing in it slightly and the beard he had begun growing the month before and that was just starting to come in right;

suits with a little space left for his Smith & Wesson nine-millimeter semiautomatic pistol in its stiff holster under his left arm. Unfortunately, he was wearing his gray pinstripe tonight.

He was standing at the door to his office, where he kept returning to watch the big man with the broken nose reading a book in the lounging area across the lobby. He was sure the man was there to take a gambling debt or a loan payment out of a guest's hide. He had seen the type often enough when he was undercover.

None of the four armed men in the lobby knew why any of the others was there.

Caudhill could see the hotel dick even if the hotel dick couldn't see him for the ferns in the lounging area, and assumed he was the one being watched. He had considered wearing a suit to blend in with his surroundings, but he never felt comfortable when so dressed—also he had never found one with a jacket that could conceal a sawed-off, his favorite weapon, without looking as if he had a pregnant rhinoceros hidden under there as well. Freedom of movement was everything in his work.

When he had been sitting for fifteen minutes he rose, stretched, and strolled over to the elevators. The uniformed man there became alert at his approach.

"There a cigarette counter in this place?" Caudhill asked.

"It's closed this time of night. Sorry, sir."

He could hear a car rumbling down the shaft. "That's okay, thanks."

He was turning away when the bell sounded indicating that the car had come to a halt at that floor. He timed his whirl with the trundling noise of the doors sliding open, unzipping his Windbreaker with one hand while swinging out the eighteen-inch shotgun with the other.

Glancing up at the sound of the bell, Sergeant Weinacre saw the stocky man zipping open his jacket as he turned and recognized the movement. He lunged to his feet, dropping his book and clawing out the Cobra.

David W. Thornton couldn't see what was going on in front of the elevators, but he saw the big broken-nosed man leap up and bring a revolver into play. He drew the Smith & Wesson from under his arm with the ease of long practice on the federal range.

Slowest to react was Leon, who saw everything from his station behind the desk: flame disgorging from the end of the shotgun in the hands of the man in the blue Windbreaker, blowing in half the security man at the elevators; the big broken-nosed man in the lounging area shouting something that was drowned out by the roar and then firing twice at Windbreaker's back; Thornton putting one into the big broken-nosed man's chest from a two-handed stance, the wind on his bullet stirring the fronds of a big fern. Leon fumbled for the Browning in his pocket, but it had slid down and turned sideways. He popped a stitch in the seam of his blazer and nearly dislocated his arm, and then he tore his pocket freeing the little .25 and almost dropped it, the nickel plating slippery in his hand.

Silence thundered down on top of the reports, which had sounded so close together they might have been one long explosion. In it, the elevator security man writhed and twitched on a carpet thick with gore, his killer on his knees over him with the shotgun held across his thighs and two bullets in his back. Weinacre lay sprawled across the settee he had recently vacated, his heels out and the revolver lying on the carpet at his feet. Thornton maintained his shooter's stance with smoke twisting out the end of the nine-millimeter's barrel. Inside the open elevator car crouched a woman in her fifties, barefoot and attired in a nightgown, who had locked herself out of her room and come down to ask for a second key. Her eyes were wide and round.

A cracking report split the silence. Thornton spun on his right foot, swinging the Smith & Wesson around in a quarter-turn. Leon stood behind the desk looking sheepish with the Browning glittering in his hand. He had fired it accidentally when the barrel collided with the edge of the desk coming up. The bullet had gone into the floor.

Picante and Michael Boniface came down a few minutes later. Picante put one foot outside the elevator door, looked, pushed his employer to the rear of the car, and pressed the button for their floor.

"Killing Sunsmith won't get your money back," Macklin said. "Anyway, you've got millions."

"It isn't the money, it's the principle."

They were in the living room of Macklin's house in Southfield. Carmen Thalberg sipped whiskey with a splash from a glass tumbler in the plaid chair Macklin had bought to replace the one his ex-wife had burned all over with cigarettes the many times she has passed out while sitting in it. This one could put it away, too; but she was on her third tumbler and hadn't dropped so much as a syllable so far, although her accent was more pronounced.

"When people say that, it's usually the money." He was sitting on the sofa nursing a whiskey-and-Pepsi highball. The clock on the mantel of the fireplace he never used read 10:57. He had been home from jail an hour.

"Women in my bracket spend as much on a weekend shopping spree in New York as he's stolen," she said. "Not me. But you'll never know what it's like to be taken for a ride like any dumb spic *puta* that came in last week on a boatload of bananas. You know what I want? I want the son of a bitch to stop and say, 'I picked the wrong broad.' That's what I want."

"That's where most shooters slip up. They want the mark to know what's happening instead of just going ahead and switching him off. You want him dead, or you want him to squirm? I don't do both."

"I don't want him dead."

"Uh-huh." He swirled his drink around. The ice cubes didn't rattle anymore.

She said, "I like the man, that's the thing. I believe in what he's doing, I mean about gambling and all. If he'd come straight to me and told me he wanted the cash to finance his crusade—"

"You'd have given it to him."

"Uh-uh. I came by my money honestly, married it. I don't believe the rich owe anyone anything, it's the American way. I'm against gambling in Detroit, but not to the tune of the money I've been investing with him in a perfectly ethical illegal business proposition. This morning he came to me and told me he's running for Congress on a platform to ban gambling everywhere in the United States. I guess the old con isn't making enough fast enough. He needs a lesson."

She outlined the lesson she had in mind while he freshened her drink and went in to the kitchen to tip some fresh ice cubes into his. By the time he returned to the living room her voice was slurring audibly. She kicked off her shoes, which she had put on for the walk from her car into his house, and he noticed that another button on her blouse had become unfastened. He could see the clasp of her champagne-colored bra.

"It's harebrained." He sat down.

"The details, maybe. What do you think of the plan?"

"He's got four bodyguards and police protection. He's a walking crowd."

"He told me today he's refusing police protection from here on in. Said he'll have enough when he declares his candidacy."

"Which according to you he'll never do."

"I think he knows the police suspect him. He's flushing out spli–spies." She scowled down at the glass in her hand.

"Thanks," he said. "The town's full of cowboys. Try one of them."

"I can afford the best. What's the most you were ever paid?"

"A hundred thousand."

She twitched her eyebrows. "You are the best."

"Just the highest."

She set down her glass on the end table next to the chair and straightened her legs to get a hand into the pocket of her skirt. He'd noticed she didn't carry a purse. He also noticed that the slit of her skirt had fallen open to expose one stockinged leg clear to the hip. From the pocket she drew a fold of paper currency. She removed the silver clip and thumbed through the bills, then handed him one.

He looked at it from both sides, then at her. "A hundred thousand and one?"

"Call it a deposit."

He poked the bill into his shirt pocket. She smiled in approval, then looked around dreamily.

"I'm too drunk to drive home," she said.

CHAPTER 15

Another funeral to attend, and Pontier wasn't sure if he could get his dress uniform to the dry cleaners and back in time.

That was his first thought when word came in Tuesday morning that Richard Weinacre had died following surgery to remove the nine-millimeter slug from his chest. He had known the sergeant slightly during his own days as a lieutenant with General Service and had pegged him then as a sluggard who coasted along drawing his time until he saw something he wanted, then scrambled to look busy—the police equivalent of an academic underachiever who crammed for exams to make up for time lost. Cops like that were dangerous, not so much because they crashed and burned sooner or later as because some worthier individual usually crashed and burned with them. In this case it was Thornton the hotel detective, whom if he were a cop and Pontier were on the shooting board, Pontier would have exonerated *prima facie*. As it was he would probably go down for involuntary manslaughter, and all because

Weinacre failed to identify himself and state his business in the lobby going in. Almost as bad, the two men he had gone there to arrest were smoke now, along with eighteen months of investigative hard work. For this he would be buried in full state with a color guard and coverage on all three local TV stations.

The hotel clerk was at County awaiting arraignment on charges of carrying a concealed weapon and illegal discharge of a firearm inside city limits. He was the one who pieced together for officers the events leading to that bloody Shakespearean scene that had greeted the first uniforms on the premises, including the fact that the unidentified man now in a coma at Detroit Receiving with two of Weinacre's slugs in his back had asked for the number of Michael Boniface's suite. The elevator security man was dead at the scene, pieces shoveled into a coroner's black rubber bag after he had inadvertently stepped in front of the shotgun. That weapon still had its serial number, but Pontier knew even as it was being checked that it would trace straight back to the factory with no stops in between. The woman in the elevator whom the shooter had mistaken for Boniface was at Receiving too, being treated for shock. It was a black day for Blue Cross.

Pontier was wondering if he should call home and ask his wife to run his dress uniform to the cleaners when Sergeant Lovelady joined him at the coffee machine. The fat detective was in his shirtsleeves and smelled of aftershave lotion and sweat.

"Give up?" Pontier handed him the cup he had just filled for himself and reached for another.

Lovelady blew on the coffee. "Getting air. He ain't talking till his lawyer gets here."

"I thought Troy Donahue in there was his lawyer."

"Stand-in for Howard Klegg."

"Christ, we're just questioning him. He isn't under arrest."

"Tell him."

The inspector found Boniface seated at the table in the interrogation room. The young lawyer was standing by the air vent smoking a cigarette. Pontier noticed the bandage over his left eyebrow and remembered the Belleville shooting. His client looked old and heavy under the harsh light, his black hair shining like shoe polish on a worn old boot. Pontier sat down.

"Mike, what's this about Klegg? You're not busted."

"That's Mr. Boniface to you," said the lawyer.

"I told you not to say my name," Boniface cut in harshly. "George, I bet these young pricks mangle yours even worse."

He had a ghastly grin that Pontier struggled to match. They hadn't met before that morning. "I guess we weren't much different when we were that age."

"Speak for yourself. When you were that age I was your age."

"Lovelady show you the pictures we took of the guy in the hospital?"

Boniface nodded. "I didn't know him from Sam's dick."

"Are you talking now?"

"I didn't like that fat-ass sergeant. He's got a face like puke."

Listen to the pot, Pontier thought. He said, "The guy in the hospital isn't on file, which doesn't surprise me. Maggiore wouldn't hire anybody local to take you out in the Pontchartrain lobby."

"Maggiore, shit. He can have this town. I'm retired."

"I thought nobody quit the organization."

The grin again. His teeth were gray, like his complexion. "That Sunday-supplement crap. We aren't like the Supreme Court. We aren't even like *us* any more. Colombians, Cubans, shit, the Arabs coming in with that blow from the Middle East, they'd pop their mothers to get the cops to vacuum their rugs for free. I'm damn glad I'm shut of it."

"Picante thinks Maggiore bought the hit."

"Picante didn't say shit. Come on, George. Maggiore's laying there at Receiving, all those tubes stuck in him watching the blood go out with his piss, he's going to worry about my health? I thought you cops might've got smarter by the time I left Milan."

"No, we're just as dumb as when we sent you up."

"I've bought better cops than you, nigger," Boniface flared.

The young lawyer stepped away from the vent. "You said my client isn't under arrest, Inspector. That means we can leave any time we want."

"Hell, I'm comfortable." Boniface undid his collar, allowing a roll of reddened flesh to settle over the knot of his necktie. "Excuse the language, George. You'd think three years inside would make a man more patient."

"I think you're impatient to have your old job back. That's why Maggiore signed a contract on you, and it's why you hired Macklin to knock him down Saturday night."

"You got Macklin in custody?"

"You've got enough lines into this department to know we released him last night."

"I haven't even seen Mac since—"

"Watch it, Mike. He came to visit you in your suite the day after you were sprung."

"I was about to say since then. It was just a friendly call. He's on his own now. I told him that was smart. Mac always did have too much upstairs to waste it cleaning up after everyone else."

"He's still doing it. Only now he's picking who he cleans up after."

"I don't know what you're talking about, of course."

"Mike, Mike." Pontier shook his head. "I don't give a shit how many of you mob guys jerk each other's chains. Somebody's got to stand up for the innocents whose lights get put out just because they're standing too close, the hotel security men and the old ladies who lock themselves out of their rooms."

"Wish I could help."

"The last person who said that in here was Maggiore's bodyguard. We tanked him for twenty-four hours."

"Go ahead. I just did three years."

The door opened and Lovelady leaned in. Pontier got up and went over.

"Klegg's here," murmured the sergeant.

"He got a writ?"

"What do you think?"

Pontier gave him a flat look. "Your mouth must have heard your brain's retiring soon."

"Sorry, Inspector. It ain't you, it's these wise-asses and their lawyers."

" 'Kay." Raising his voice: "You're out of here, Boniface."

Boniface rose, buttoning his collar. "What happened to Mike?"

"Just take your ass out of my interrogation room."

"Inspector, your attitude—" the lawyer began.

"And take that piece of legal shit you're trailing with you."

Boniface paused on his way out. He looked like an old Italian fruit peddler on his way to a funeral.

"I've been gone better than two hours. If my dog messed up the carpet I guess the department will take care of the hotel cleaning bill."

"With you up there, who'll notice?" Pontier held the door for him.

The sunlight woke Macklin finally.

He usually came to consciousness with the same thought he had taken to bed the night before, but forty-eight hours in Holding and Interrogation had come down hard on him in the night and for a few minutes he lay there trying to figure out who was the naked woman lying with her legs intertwined with his. She smelled faintly of him and, not so faintly, of half-digested whiskey. With that discovery his memory kicked in. Carefully he disentangled himself and slid out from under the sheet. Carmen turned over on her back and began snoring. Her hair looked lighter in the morning light, her skin dark against the rumpled sheets.

The electric alarm on the bedstand read ten o'clock. He hadn't slept that late in months. He dressed as quietly as possible, leaning against the wall to pull on his trousers. Something rustled while he was buttoning his shirt and he took a folded dollar bill out of the pocket.

Standing there holding up his pants with one hand and the bill in the other, he thought: A dollar and a fuck. Next it'll be chocolate bars.

CHAPTER 16

Dr. Stepp took three minutes removing each of the two bullets from Charles Maggiore's upper thorax and two hours repairing the damage they had made going in and the damage he had made going in after them. From the operating room the patient was returned to Intensive Care, where an infection developed Tuesday night and Stepp was called in early Wednesday morning to open him up again and drain off the pus. The fever broke that afternoon, and Wednesday night a nurse awakened Gordy in the waiting room outside Surgery to report that his employer's prognosis for recovery was excellent. Gordy thanked her and asked when he could see him.

"He's under sedation. Why don't you go home and get some rest and come back tomorrow?"

"I ain't paid to rest."

He slept in the waiting room that night, as he had been doing since his release from the Wayne County Jail. Another nurse who had failed to make him heed visiting hours had threatened to call Security, but when he rose to meet a doctor who had stepped in to monitor the situation the doctor had smiled weakly and said that he didn't think visiting hours applied to the waiting room. Gordy hadn't been home since the night he had discovered his employer in a bloody and unconscious condition on the floor of his gym.

On Thursday morning, a different nurse roused him from a copy of *Psychology Today* and told him Maggiore was asking for him.

The Sicilian had been moved from Intensive Care to a private room two floors up. Gordy didn't recognize either of the two uniformed police officers stationed outside the door, who studied his identification and handed it back up to him without comment. On his way inside he heard one of them say, "What would you have done if he wasn't who he said he was?"

Maggiore was lying on his back with a clear plastic tube up his nose and another tube taped to his left arm feeding him liquid from a bottle suspended upside-down over the bed. He was gray under his tan and his hump looked bigger than usual under the white hospital gown. He looked at Gordy and said, "Jesus, you look worse than me."

Although he had been washing in a public rest room down the hall from the waiting area, Gordy hadn't changed his clothes or shaved since jail. His suit was wrinkled, one lapel stained with sauce from the spaghetti he had eaten two days earlier in the hospital commissary. He made no reply to the comment.

"Door closed?"

Gordy went over and closed it.

"How dead is Boniface?"

"Not very."

"What the fuck happened?"

Gordy told him about the shoot-out in the Pontchartrain lobby.

"That son of a bitch Constable. Get him here."

"How you feeling?"

"Like I been shot twice, how the fuck you think I feel? I guess the cops must be heating up the town."

"I don't know. I been here."

"All the time? Jesus."

"Well, I did jail for a night. That Inspector Pontier."

"That black bastard."

"My ears are burning. You fellows talking about me?"

Pontier had made no noise opening the door. He was wearing a brown pinstriped suit that emphasized his long leanness. Sergeant Lovelady, broad and dumpy in his yellow sportcoat, closed the door behind him and stood in front of it. Maggiore said, "That's the trouble with hospitals. You can't pick who visits you."

"I heard you were conscious. I thought you might be in a mood to answer a couple of questions. You know, to find out if there's brain damage."

"I'm starting to feel weak. Gordy, get the nurse."

When the bodyguard turned, Pontier placed spread fingers against his wrinkled shirt. "You must be getting your shooters on sale at K-Mart," he told Maggiore. "That lobby shoot has to be the sloppiest since St. Valentine's Day in Chicago."

"I heard about it. One of those drug things."

"Listen, no one's mad at you. Boniface tried you, it's just natural you'd try him back. But a cop and a citizen got killed and somebody's got to pay the cashier."

"Gordy says you busted the hotel dick."

"He was a bystander too."

"I don't like it when a cop gets killed any more than you. It's bad business and it rubs off on everybody. But you're shouting down the wrong hole here."

"Anyway, it's not why I came. The line to take you down forms behind the Justice Department, there's plenty of time for that. Let's talk about the Reverend Sunsmith."

"Jesus, we covered that."

"Yeah, but that was before I knew you were one of his angels."

"No jokes, please, Inspector. I got more stitches in me than a boccie ball."

"I'll save you the time and energy it takes to deny it. We've got it in writing, complete with your signature on the bottom. You've been donating regularly for the past year. You're a generous gangster, Maggiore. You ought to hire a press agent to tell the world how generous you are."

"Just because I got excommunicated doesn't mean I don't still believe in God."

"Thing is, if you'd told me you were a contributor the last time I asked you about Sunsmith, I might not have wasted so much time suspecting you of buying the contract on him. I wonder why you didn't."

"I'm a private man. My religious beliefs are my business."

"Bullshit. Your business beliefs are your religion."

Maggiore said nothing.

"Detroit is famous for its churches," Pontier went on. "After cars and murders and crooked politicians they have to be the first thing people think of when they hear the name. A cop has to wonder why you'd pick Sunsmith's to finance, him being so hot against gambling and you with so much of your capital tied up in casino equipment. You had to stand to gain enough to make up for all that gall you had to be swallowing."

Maggiore kept silent. He looked genuinely weak now.

Pontier said, "All the gold's been dug up and you can't speculate in oil anymore. The last way left to make quick free cash is to cheat Uncle Sam. The dummy company you've been contributing through has been pulling in dividends from the Reverend's operation without declaring them.

"What you maybe don't know is that you weren't the only one to stumble over this particular gold mine. There are at least six others involved. It doesn't take Einstein to figure Sunsmith doesn't bring enough in on his collection plate to make all those investors happy. So he's robbing St. Peter to pay St. Paul."

"Sort of like a chain letter," suggested Lovelady, near the door.

"Call it Sunsmith's Epistle to the Pigeons." Pontier studied the man in the bed. "Yeah, you knew it. That's why you hired the hit on the Reverend."

"I told you why I didn't."

"It sounded good at the time, too. But this new development is my ball and I'm running with it. I lied before; I want you for that dead cop. But if I can't get you for that I'll settle for conspiracy to commit on Sunsmith."

The door opened and Dr. Stepp entered. His youthful face was dark. "Gentlemen, this isn't a press conference."

Pontier was still looking at Maggiore. "Next time I'll bring flowers. With a warrant wrapped around them."

Gordy hung back.

"You too," said the surgeon. "Your boss is a mile from out of the woods."

"Go home," said Maggiore.

The big bodyguard hovered. "You sure?"

"I got babysitters up the ass. Right, Doc?"

"Next they'll be strip-searching the nurses." Stepp's tone was not bantering.

"I'll be back tomorrow," Gordy said.

"Get Constable," the Sicilian reminded him.

When Gordy returned the next morning, shaved and dressed in a fresh black suit and crisp white shirt and accompanied by the neat pale man in yellow, Maggiore was sitting up in bed. The tube in his nose has been removed but he still had the other in his arm. Near the foot of the bed, completely filling an easy chair with a steel frame and orange vinyl upholstery, sat the Reverend Thomas Aquinas Sunsmith. He had on a charcoal-gray suit and vest with a maroon knitted tie on an eggshell shirt.

"I never thought I'd be dressed louder than the Reverend," commented Constable after a moment.

Maggiore said, "He's incognito. Six-three and three hundred pounds of it."

He stood to wrap a great brown hand around Constable's small neat white one. "The officers didn't want to let me pass at first," he rumbled. "Mr. Maggiore persuaded them. I had to send the elders home."

Gordy stationed himself in front of the door and said nothing. He had five inches and twelve pounds on the Reverend, but the latter's reflectionless black eyes were disturbing.

"It's fortunate that we're here at the same time," Sunsmith told Constable.

"Wait'll you hear it," Maggiore said.

Said Sunsmith, "I've arranged a rally in Hart Plaza the day before the referendum to place casino gambling on the November ballot. It will be covered by all three local television stations and my own cable network. I plan to announce then."

"Announce?" Constable was looking up at him.

"My candidacy for the U.S. House of Representatives from this district. There will be a vacancy in November and I plan to fill it."

Constable tried to make a joke out of it. "Well, you're big enough."

The black eyes were immobile in the smooth round face. They looked as if they would retain thumbprints. "A campaign donation of fifty thousand dollars would start me off in a competitive condition."

"That's the part I wanted to hear," Maggiore said.

"The arrangement has been monetary so far," continued the Reverend. "We're opposed on the sin of gambling, but apart from that we are of much the same mind on legislation affecting business and the church. I would personally represent our interests in Washington."

"Well." Constable didn't know what else to say.

"How do we know you won't introduce some asshole legislation to outlaw gambling coast-to-coast?" Maggiore wanted to know. "We got interests in Vegas and Atlantic City."

"I will always be opposed to the practice. But I'll be busy enough halting its spread without trying to reverse what's been done. A soul lost to Satan is irredeemable. Meanwhile I won't forget the believers who helped put me in office. I see no reason why our arrangement should change simply because I'll be trading the pulpit for the lectern."

"That was money. Now you're talking influence. Money you can count. I got a judge and half-interest in a senator now. Where do I gain?"

"A vote in the other house."

Maggiore scratched his hump, something he wouldn't have done outside the hospital. "Try me again after the referendum. I can only think about one ballot at a time."

"I hope you'll be in a mood to hear what I have to say."

"Well, that depends on how the vote comes out, doesn't it?"

The Reverend shrugged, displacing as much air with the movement as a foreign car rolling over. "Campaign funds have started coming in. I can't say how long the offer will stand."

"I live to take chances."

Sunsmith took his dignity from the room. The room seemed much bigger without him. When the door closed, Maggiore looked at the blank television screen suspended from the ceiling. "I wouldn't vote for that fat nigger if he ran against Mussolini."

"Why didn't you tell him that?" asked Constable.

"You heard him; fucker's got a pulpit. With his hard-on against gambling I wouldn't lay it past him to tip our whole deal just for spite. IRS's got a lien on my personal holdings now. They slap one on the company's too I won't be able to hire a first-year law student for the other stuff. Where'd you get that piece of shit that shot up the Pontchartrain?"

"Toledo swore by him."

"You swore by that pair that fucked up in Belleville last week. What good are you, Phil? I'd turn you out and plug in Gordy there if he didn't put so much store in other people's breathing."

Constable unbuttoned his jacket. "I can run the straight business for you or I can interview killers. Doing both isn't easy."

"Turn the business over to that expensive cunt you got sitting in the outer office."

"You know I can't do that."

"Find me some talent. The real thing, not some sticks cowboy with no more brains than you can fire out of a sawed-off. I don't care if you got to go clear back to Sicily, just don't get me no more fuck-ups."

"The police will be watching Boniface now. It'll cost."

"Fuck Boniface. He can wait. You got two weeks and four days to find a button worth pushing. That's the day of the gambling referendum. No matter which way that vote goes, I want Sunsmith hit. I want him cut up in so many pieces God will have to send back for instructions to put him back together."

CHAPTER 17

By Monday it had gotten really hard to avoid calling the suite.

During his lunch with Picante, Roger Macklin had seen no problem in agreeing to wait for Boniface's lieutenant to call him. But after a week he had started wondering if he had been passed over in favor of someone the Reverend wouldn't recognize. He didn't have cable, but on Sunday he had listened to Sunsmith's sermon on the radio, half expecting to hear gunshots. That the services had concluded without mishap was small comfort. Roger had spent the hundred dollars Picante had advanced him upon parting company and if the telephone didn't ring soon he would have to start stuffing bags at Kroger's. Had he known there was so much waiting involved he might have chosen some other business. It rang while he was wondering if he should chance going out for cigarettes.

"Roger? Me. The fountain." The line clicked.

He replaced the receiver, tingling.

Despite the recent addition of an artistic monstrosity of a waterworks in Hart Plaza, to longtime Detroiters there was only one fountain. It stood on one end of an elongated strip of real estate named Belle Isle in the middle of the Detroit River, where in the gathering dusk Roger could see its spray glittering in red and blue light the moment his tires hit the narrow bridge leading to the island from Jefferson Avenue. He found a space in the public lot and walked in that direction, enjoying the cool air and the mist on his face. He hadn't been shut in so long since rehab.

He was sorry to learn he had beaten Picante there. Belle Isle was a favorite drop spot for local pushers and his veins throbbed with the knowledge of business transactions going on in the bushes. He wondered if he would ever be free of the longing. The only time he didn't think about it was when he was actually pulling the trigger on someone. The adrenalin rush alone compared to that feeling of supreme contentment that accompanied the needle's withdrawal.

When he made his appearance, Picante wasn't hard to spot. He was the only person near the fountain wearing a brown polyester suit and skinny necktie. The colored lights reflecting off his features filled in the hollows, making him look a little less like an ambulatory corpse.

"Hell of a sight, huh," he said in greeting. "By daylight it's plastered with pigeon shit and there's crap floating around in the water. I figure God invented nighttime after He got through with us and took a good look. You carrying?"

"On Belle Isle after dark? You bet your ass." The water was starting to run off Roger's face.

Picante motioned him away from the fountain and turned his back to the men and women in short sleeves and halters loitering nearby, shielding Roger with the movement. "Let's see."

"Right here?"

"What's the matter, it strapped to your dick?"

Roger pulled his T-shirt out of his jeans to expose the butt of the Colt Woodsman.

"Christ. You hunting doves or what?"

"It's a pro piece."

"Sure, you're sitting in the back seat, the mark's behind the wheel, you tell him pull over, you put one in the back of his head. How you fixing to get Sunsmith in a car with you in back? Let's take a walk."

Roger covered the butt and accompanied the older man back to the parking lot, where they waited for two men seated in the front of a Buick Riviera to finish their business and take off walking in separate directions before Picante led the way to a brown car parked in the shade of a lilac bush. He unlocked the door on the passenger's side, reached under the dash, and freed a newspaper-wrapped package from the tangled wiring with a tearing sound of tape. From the package he unrolled a square, steel-colored semiautomatic pistol and held it out butt first for Roger to take. It was heavy.

"Forty-five?" He turned it over in his hands. It had a cherrywood grip and no serial number or place where a serial number had been.

"Forty-five mag."

"Jesus."

"Dirty Harry's out of date," Picante said. "*This* is the most powerful handgun in the world. Man like Sunsmith, you probably won't get a chance for more than one shot. With this it's all you'll need."

"My dad always said stay away from automatics."

"That's just because they leave shell casings behind. With this it won't matter, because you'll be leaving the gun behind with them. It's a prototype, no serial number or manufacturer's identification plate. Cops'll go crazy trying to trace it past where you dropped it."

"So where do I drop it?"

"Hart Plaza, high noon, two weeks from today."

Roger grinned to show he got the joke. Picante's face was a black oval in the darkness. He couldn't tell if he was grinning back.

"Bring your guts," Picante added.

CHAPTER 18

Carmen Thalberg said Sunsmith had his suits and robes tailored in a little shop over a tattoo parlor on Montcalm. She remembered that he had worn a particularly arresting cucumber-colored three-piece during one of his visits and had taken literally her shocked inquiry into its source.

The shop's entrance was on an alley, from which Macklin climbed a steep flight of squeaking, rubber-runnered stairs and followed a wainscoted hallway through an open door into a big room smelling of fabric and sizing. A high wooden counter separated him from rows of racks supporting suits and tuxedoes in all colors and patterns and bolts of material stacked like fireplace logs under the back windows. He rang the customer bell on the counter. After a minute a gray-haired Korean in shirtsleeves and a vest emerged from the jungle of wool and silk.

"I'm an elder with the Reverend Sunsmith's church," Macklin said. "He asked me to stop by and find out when's his next fitting."

The Korean drew a black-bound notebook from his shirt pocket and leafed through it, licking his thumb in between pages. "No fitting. New red robe ready Tuesday." He closed the book.

"Okay, I'll pick it up then."

The Korean looked at him unblinkingly. "You new?"

"Why?"

"Reverend he pick up his own clothes. Good smell here, he says."

"Oh."

"New color too," the Korean said, squinting. "White elders, what next?"

Macklin left the shop. Sometimes it was easier than other times. Those were the times he trusted least.

He had lunch in Greektown and drove from there to a trailer park in Romulus, where a black weapons dealer he knew only as Sooty offered him three MAC-10 semiautomatic pistols converted to full auto for two thousand the package, fifty-round magazines included. Macklin asked him what he had in revolvers.

"Revolvers, shit, I can do him two-fifties, grenade launchers in case lots, man wants high-top shoes." Sooty scratched his great melon belly, brown and hairless where his white T-shirt ended and suspended over khaki trousers worn through at the knees. "I'm showing what's on the block this week. You want to special-order, I don't guarantee the pieces you get didn't blow down some clerk in a convenience store job Friday night. I'm talking virgin timber here, spray twenty rounds a fucking second."

"Where are they?"

"Man, you're leaning on them."

Sooty occupied the only seat not supporting a box or a wooden case. Macklin was standing with one arm resting on a fiberboard carton stenciled GOLD COAST ORANGES, on top of a kitchen table littered with machine screws and recoil springs.

Macklin said, "I don't know why you haven't been busted before this."

"I got a wait list with more gold badges on it than seven A.M. roll call at thirteen hundred. You got anything against magnums?"

"Not if it's all you've got."

"I can let you have a .357 for five hundred, two-fifty if you put up the two large for the MAC-10s."

"Christ, I hate full autos twice as much as semi-autos. One two-second burst and you're out of business."

"So reconvert them, pull the sear blocks and replace the pins. I can do that for you."

"You're in a big hurry to get out from under them. It looks like."

The black man belched. "I'm running a clearance. Got me a boat in the De-troit River, the *John Brown*, thirty-two-foot cabin cruiser. Come November, man, I'm out the St. Lawrence and down the Coast peddling Uzis to the monkey-jumpers in Nicaragua. No more of these fucking Michigan winters for me."

"You won't be able to cut the same deal with the Coast Guard. They've got sources on both shores."

"I got two direct-feed Rolls Royces and a turbo backup. They can try and run me down."

"Two grand for the lot. I'll do the reconverting myself."

"Man, I didn't get this fat dishing soup out the back door."

"MAC-10s were going three-sixty a pop last time I looked," Macklin said. "The mag ran you a buck and a half. You stand to clear close to a thousand my way. Not too shabby."

"Hunnert-fifty for a mag, you'll never see that day again." Sooty grinned, showing his tongue in the gap where his top teeth were missing. "I got to get it. It ain't here."

Macklin figured he had his entire stock on the premises. But he was used to the stall. Sooty would use the time to check his references. "Tomorrow night okay?"

"Yeah, I like night."

Dusk found Macklin on the top floor of a new pinecone-shaped high-rise in Windsor, watching the river slowly turn from pink to green to black as the Detroit skyline swallowed the sun. The room was nearly as large as the floor plan of his house, with a burnt-orange shag carpet and black-and-chromium furniture and abstract watercolors on the walls. A spider-shaped contraption of a fixture clung to the ceiling, shedding soft yellow light from copper funnels.

Behind the bar, a man whose Miami tan contrasted sharply with his thinning white hair stood measuring bourbon from a shot glass into a tumbler of milk. He had fine, clean-shaven features and a powder-blue silk shirt stuffed loosely into the tops of black wool trousers and might have been taken for a born aristocrat but for his hands. They were large and red-knuckled with old dirt in the creases.

"Doctor's orders," he explained, when he caught Macklin watching him. "He said milk was the thing for my herniated esophagus, but I put myself through business school working for a dairy farmer and I can't stand the smell. This is the only way I can bring myself to drink it."

His Yiddish accent was almost inaudible. Most who noticed it mistook it for German. Macklin remembered when it was much heavier, when his father worked in the junkyard owned by the man and the man's two brothers. It wasn't a junkyard now but a hotel downtown, and none of those who stayed there knew they were living on top of half a dozen victims of what the Prohibition press had called the Little Jewish Mafia. The man's name was Hermann.

He offered to serve Macklin, whose first inclination was to decline. But dimly in his memory glimmered an old-world rule about accepting a man's hospitality in his house, a rule that for Hermann would still be fresh. "Hold the milk," Macklin said.

The old man brought over a tumbler like his own, with

water and ice substituted for milk. The hand with which he proffered the drink was as steady as the building. He watched his guest take a sip before seating himself in the chair opposite. He drank, whisked away the moustache with a crooked finger, and set the glass into a depression built into the arm of the chair at his right elbow.

"How long, Peter?"

Hermann was one of the few who called him by his Christian name. "Since my father's funeral," he said. "Fourteen years."

"Fourteen years. Divided into seventy it is not long. You've aged."

"Well, if I had to choose."

The corners of the old man's lips twitched. It might have been a tic. "He was a good man, dependable. That time those two guinea punks had my brother David pinned against the cash register, they were going to cut his manhood because he wouldn't pay them not to, your father drove a Kenworth cab right through the window. Afterwards my other brother Simon wanted to charge him for the damage to the headlights and grille and the office, take it out of his salary. We talked him out of it. David gave your father a raise and a nice coin purse made out of one of the guineas' scrotums. I wonder what happened to it."

Macklin said he didn't know.

"Bad times." Hermann picked up his glass. "One thing, you knew who your enemies were then. Italian against Jew, Polack against Ukrainian, and all of them against the Greeks. Now all these *shvartzes,* spics, oy, Arabs, who knows how those animals think? We're all mixed together now and a Jew could get his throat cut by another Jew as quick as by anyone else. Look at you, a good Scotch lad, working for the wops."

"I'm working for myself these days."

"You sell your loyalty on the street like a whore, no one's blaming you. You're forced to it. Simon would be spinning in his grave if he had one instead of a hundred pounds of concrete on the bottom of Lake Erie."

Macklin smelled another story brewing. "At the funeral, you told me I had a favor coming if I ever needed one," he said quickly.

Hermann swirled the pale liquid in his glass. "He wanted better for you, your father did. He had your life all mapped out from your christening. You were going to break Babe Ruth's home run record before you were thirty and then you were going to run for senator. He wanted to make sure you were presidential material by the time you turned thirty-five and became eligible." He drank, touched his lip. Slowly the pupils of his faded blue eyes opened to let in the present. "What is it you want?"

Macklin said, "I want to kidnap someone."

CHAPTER 19

The building, in the warehouse district two blocks east of the Renaissance Center, had been used to store liquor during the dry time, then machine parts after Repeal. In the sixties Hermann had had it converted to offices, but it had been empty for ten years, the last five of which the former junk magnate had spent in a legal hammerlock with members of the urban planning commission who wanted to condemn it. It was blackened brick with big segmented windows paneled over during renovation and a soundproofed second floor that had been a dance studio complete with a fifteen-foot brass *barre* and a pale rectangle on the hardwood floor where a piano had stood. Macklin tested the soundproofing by tossing a string of lit firecrackers into the big room and shutting the door against the noise, leaned all his weight on the *barre* without managing to loosen the bolts where it was fastened to the wall, and pronounced the place perfect.

The next morning, Wednesday, he had the lights turned back on and installed bars on the windows and a deadbolt lock on the door leading to the hallway just in case the *barre* didn't hold. He spent the afternoon reporting to Carmen, part of it in bed, and later he went back to the trailer park to complete his transaction with Sooty. From there he returned to the dance studio in order to meet the men Hermann had sent over.

There were three of them. He knew them by nicknames only, and they knew him by no name at all. Two were black. One of them, called Deac, had done twenty-seven months in Marquette for his part in an armored car robbery with three other blacks who called themselves the Nairobi Army of Liberty. He was nearly as big as any of the Reverend's elders, wore his hair in a mohawk, and strung himself with a rainbow of beads over a denim jacket cut off at the shoulders to show off the muscles in his arms and the head of a water buffalo tattooed on his left bicep with N.A.L. blocked between its horns. The other black man, Ski, was as tall as Deac but at least a hundred pounds lighter, straight up and down with no hips in black jeans held up with suspenders under a tan silk jacket that hung on him like a bath towel. His hair had been straightened and combed into a glossy pompadour and he had on wraparound sunglasses that completely hid his eyes. The Willow Run police had arrested him for the blowtorch murder of a city councilman, but the case had been thrown out of court when no witnesses came forward.

"Why do they call you Ski?" Macklin asked him. "You sure aren't Polish."

His grin lent him a close resemblance to Stevie Wonder. " 'Cause when I walks I slides."

Macklin reached up and removed the dark glasses. Ski's pupils shrank in the sudden exposure to light. "Use?"

"Reefer now and again. Tried snorting coke once but I almost drowned." He giggled, a soft bubbling sound.

"Lay off that shit while I'm paying you."

The giggling stopped. The grin fell away. "I hear you."

Macklin gave him back his glasses.

The white man in the trio was five-seven and wide, not fat, with thin brown hair combed straight forward down the slope of his forehead and eyes set far enough apart to lay a hand between without touching either. They were brown and looked like thin paper circles pasted on. His face was unadorned and unblemished and unmemorable but for the eyes. He was wearing a brown jacket with snaps and a brown sportshirt tucked into brown double-knit trousers. Brown wingtips on his feet. Noticing him at all required effort. Macklin made it. "You're Hank?"

"I guess I must be."

"What've you done?"

"Nothing you've heard about."

His voice had all the inflection of a dial tone.

"No sheet?"

He shook his head.

"Indulge me."

"Chile, 1974. El Salvador, 1982. Grenada, 1983. India, 1984."

"CIA?"

"Same thing. Other letters."

"Why'd you quit?"

"I was starting to forget English."

"What were you doing between 1974 and 1982?"

"Recovering." He unbuttoned his shirt to the belt buckle and pulled it open. His abdomen was a relief map of healed-over scars.

"Shrapnel?"

"M-16." He snorted. "One of ours. They took out a kidney and four feet of gut and stuck me in charge of Central American requisitions for eight years."

"Anything against automatic weapons because of it?"

"Not as long as I'm behind them." He redid the buttons.

"What do you think of the MAC-10?"

"Kiddie shit. But it does its job."

Macklin stepped away to address the group. "No killing on this one. If someone stops breathing the lady stops paying."

"Lady?" Ski was grinning again.

"You'll meet her later. Hermann tell you the job?"

Deac said, "We snatch somebody."

Macklin took from a window ledge a sheaf of flyers he had found in one of the reading rooms that the Reverend Sunsmith's church maintained throughout the city and handed one to each of the three. They contained passages from the Bible on the sin of greed and on the lots cast for Jesus' robe. Each included a picture of Sunsmith in his robes behind a pulpit with a life-size bronze cast of Christ on the cross at his back. "Recognize him?"

"Them holes in his hands and feet rings a bell," Ski said.

"You know who I mean."

"Yeah, I know him. Heavy shit."

"He comes back here alive and he stays until the lady says he goes. Anybody have any problems with that?"

"How we get him away from his bodyguards?" Deac asked.

"We take them too."

"You mean breathing?"

"You heard what I said about that."

Hank said, "What's it pay?"

"Ten thousand apiece, guaranteed. If no one gets killed."

Ski touched his sunglasses. "Well, it'll be something new."

"You're in?"

"Shit. Yeah, I'm in."

"Hank?"

"Where and when's this go down?"

"Tomorrow, in an alley off Montcalm."

"I got to see the plan first."

"Uh-uh. This isn't one of Sunsmith's reading rooms. The literature stays here."

"How do I know you're not some cracker thinks he's James Bond with a hard-on?"

"How do I know you didn't get those belly scars bending over a barbed-wire fence to pick your toes?"

"Because Hermann told you different."

"That's right."

The brown eyes were flat and reflected no light. "Yeah, I get you. Count me."

Macklin looked at Deac, who shrugged, bunching the muscles atop his great shoulders. Taking that as his answer, Macklin turned and tossed his keys to Ski, who caught them against his chest.

"Green Camaro behind the building. There's a box in the trunk. Don't drop it."

Ski twirled the ring around his right index finger, let it fly into a steep arc that brushed the high paneled ceiling, and caught it in his left hand. Then he went out. Five minutes later he returned carrying a fiberboard box and set it on the floor. Macklin opened it and stepped back while the three separated the flat black hand-held automatics and twelve-inch magazines from the excelsior inside. Hank had his together and a round jacked into the chamber inside of three seconds. Then he undid it and repeated the maneuver more slowly for the others. They had theirs ready to fire a minute later.

Macklin said, "I was going to turn them back to semiauto, but we might have to spray some lead in order to get the bodyguards' attention. Hank, that'll be your job if we need it. Those things are harder to control than the heavier automatics."

"Not if you know what you're doing."

"No killing, remember. If it goes sour we split."

"What's the matter, you don't like red?"

Macklin drew the nickel-plated .357 magnum from under his jacket and shot Hank in the left eye. The bullet took off the back of his skull and tore into the soundproofed wall behind him. His finger tightened convulsively on the MAC-10's trigger as his knees folded. The gun spat out an empty shell casing and jammed. The shell bounced on the floor with a tapping noise in the silence following the revolver's roar. Hank fell the rest of the way onto his face.

Ski and Deac fumbled with their weapons.

"Don't bother," Macklin said. "Yours are loaded with empties just like his. You get live rounds later."

Ski said, "You said no killing."

"On the job. This was a favor I did for Hermann in return for you two and the use of the hall. Hank was getting set to cut a deal with the feds for his old job back."

"A hit. Jesus Christ."

"I figured as long as I had to do it anyway it might as well count for something. I'll kill the first one of you that departs from the script."

Deac said, "What about the stiff?"

"Hermann's sending a clean-up crew. Either of you want to walk?"

Ski grinned. "Man, we just watched you dust a dude. You ain't going to turn out either one of us, so why ask?"

"Just testing for team spirit."

"We're short a man," Deac said.

"A man maybe."

Deac and Ski turned to watch the slim tawny brown-haired woman coming in the door. She had on an olive-drab jumpsuit and worn hiking boots that laced up her ankles with the trousers bloused out above the tops.

"You'll call her Carmen," Macklin told them. "She'll be driving the crash car."

Ski had lost his grin when the women entered. Now it flickered. "A broad? Shit."

Macklin belted his magnum and squatted to pick up Hank's MAC-10 from the floor where it had dropped. Standing, he handed it to Carmen, whose face had paled infinitesimally under its dark pigment in the presence of the corpse.

She hesitated only a second, then released the gun's magazine with a flick of her thumb, ran back the action to clear the jammed shell casing, and reassembled the weapon. She was nearly as fast at it as Hank had been.

"She comes from a country where every little kid can grow up to be a revolutionary general," said Macklin. "If she lived in Kansas she'd know how to operate a twelve-bottom plow. And she can drive."

"Jesus Christ," Ski said again.

Macklin said nothing. At his feet, the spreading blood from Hank's broken head, slowing now, stained the corner of the picture of the Reverend standing in front of the great crucifix.

CHAPTER 20

Sergeant Lovelady hadn't slept with his wife in eight years.

They had plenty of affection for each other. Together they had put a son and a daughter through college, adopted a Vietnamese refugee girl when they were both past forty, and started the long torturous path of special education when the girl proved to be severely retarded. But after twenty-four years of marriage the sergeant's tendency to sprawl all over both the bed and his partner had overcome their fears and hesitations and he had moved into one of the children's old bedrooms for purposes of sleeping. Unfortunately, when the telephone rang late Wednesday night it caught him sharing his wife's bed for another purpose entirely. She lifted the receiver on the eleventh ring, listened, and handed it over without comment.

"Lovelady?"

"Yeah, Inspector."

"You okay? You sound like you've been running."

"I work out sometimes. What's up?"

"It just occurred to me who's trying to kill Sunsmith."

The sergeant was aware of his wife's scrutiny. His ear felt hot. He changed hands on the receiver. "Maggiore?"

"No, his life's complicated enough just now without that. Try Mike Boniface."

"He don't know shit about gambling. I bet he votes against it. If he's registered."

"That's what I mean. We've been approaching this thing all wrong. The last thing the pro-gamblers want is for the Reverend to get whacked in the middle of a campaign against gambling. That'd slide all the undecideds into his camp. It's what the guy who signed the contract on him is counting on."

"I don't know, it don't sound like Boniface. His thinking ain't that bent."

"That's Boniface B.M."

"B.M?" He changed hands again.

"Before Milan. The slam's the strongest attitude adjustment I know."

"Well, who signed the contract on Maggiore?"

Pontier hesitated. "I'm still working on that part."

"Thanks for sharing it, Inspector."

"You sure you're all right? I've heard busted radiators that sounded better."

Lovelady said he was fine and they said good night. He handed the receiver back to his wife. "Where were we?"

"Breaking the mood." She cradled it.

CHAPTER 21

The Reverend Thomas Aquinas Sunsmith confessed privately to one material weakness, and that was his weakness for material. If requested to abandon his jewelry or his church or even his guitar in the name of his faith he would not have hesitated to comply; but should the mandate include his suits and robes he would have felt something of Job's burden. His musician's spirit quenched itself in reds and purples and pinks and cool pastels and no woman's naked flesh compared to the sensation of raw silk and virgin wool sliding between his calloused fingertips. Outside his church the only place where he felt truly close to his God was in the little second-floor tailor's shop on Montcalm.

Kwan Duc waited on him personally, unlocking the door to the fitting room with a little bow while the four elders waited outside in the hallway. Once inside he took off his coat and vest and hung them up, then slipped into the satin cardinal-colored robe, carefully avoiding looking at his reflection in the three-way mirrors until he had it fastened.

When he did look, he almost stepped back away from the flames of hell that leapt from the play of light over the glossy material. He planned to wear it at the rally in Hart Plaza a week from Monday, when he would summon forth all the brimstone at his command to condemn the gambling measure up for referendum the next day.

He stepped out of the fitting room, towering and broad and very red in the natural light coming through the windows. Kwan Duc fussed about him, smoothing creases and tugging at pouches and flipping the skirt this way and that to see how it hung. He had the Reverend raise his arms and rotate them at the shoulders and scampered about him, muttering to himself in Korean when he bent to remove a pin from the hem.

"Shoulders tight?"

"No, they're fine."

"Too long, I think."

"Not at all. It should just brush the floor."

"More yoke, maybe."

"I don't want to look like Darth Vader."

"Satisfy?"

He admired himself once more in the standing mirror inside the counter. Then he unbuttoned the robe and took it off, standing there in salmon-colored shirt and electric blue tie with matching stripes, and handed it to the Oriental. "Wrap it."

It was returned to him a few minutes later in a long white box tied with string, along with instructions to hang it as soon as he got home. Carrying the box under one arm, the Reverend went out into the hallway and descended the staircase to the street with two of the elders in front of him and the other two following behind.

The cream stretch and two-tone Buick Electra all but filled the alley. The Reverend handed the box to one of the elders to avoid crumpling it while he got into the back of the limousine, then accepted it and laid it lovingly across his lap while the elder who had been holding the door for him closed it and climbed behind the wheel. Another got in beside him in front and the others boarded the Buick. The procession started rolling.

A white van squirted across the mouth of the alley and halted with a shriek of tires, bouncing on its frame. At the same instant the door on the passenger's side sprang open and a middle-aged man with thinning dark hair and a tired face threw a leg out onto the pavement and leveled a shiny revolver at the limousine's windshield.

By that time the elder behind the wheel was already in action. He threw the limousine into reverse and rammed the smaller car behind, popping the hood and flushing a shower of steam from the radiator. The Reverend's forehead struck the back of the front seat with a noise like a basketball bounding off a padded wall. Reacting more slowly, the driver of the damaged Buick reversed, then braked squealingly when a city garbage truck came trundling up the alley behind it and stopped with a hydraulic whoosh. The cab doors flew wide and a black man bounded out each side bearing a weapon whose long straight clip advertised it as an automatic. The elder seated next to the driver flung open his door and strained out, twisting to free his 9-millimeter from under his coat. One of the blacks, big and bulgy-muscled with his hair cut like a crazy Indian's, sprayed the rear of the Buick in a short burst that sounded like one long report. The elder swore later he saw the bullets come splattering out roman-candle fashion as they shattered the taillights and pounded across the lid of the trunk. Quickly the elder laid his own weapon in plain sight on the Buick's roof and threw up his hands.

The elder driving the limousine froze with his hand inside his coat, staring through the windshield at the tired face of the man from the van and the muzzle of the shiny revolver in front of it. The man's attention was entirely on the driver.

"Shoot him, for chrissake," the driver said, just loud enough for the elder seated next to him to hear.

His partner said, "Fuck you." He was looking beyond the man, at the woman in a jumpsuit standing on a step-plate or something on the other side of the van with her arms resting on the roof and her hands wrapped around the butt and forepiece of an automatic pistol. Her light hair was pinned behind her head, and rising head and shoulders above the van like she was she looked ten feet tall.

It took almost five minutes to get the four bodyguards and Sunsmith out of the cars and disarmed and herded into their prearranged places, the Reverend and one of his men in the van with Macklin guarding them and the other three into the garbage truck's empty dump-box under Deac's gun. Sunsmith came out hugging the box he had carried out of the shop and Ski took it away from him, suspecting it contained a weapon. He whistled when he saw the scarlet robe and slipped it on over his blue turtleneck and gray cords. It hung in drapes from his slender frame and flapped about his heels as he mounted the driver's seat of the truck carrying his MAC-10. The Reverend lunged for the box after it was torn from his arms, only to howl and stagger back into the arms of one of the elders when Deac slashed the muzzle of his own pistol down the side of the Reverend's skull, opening a cut four inches long that dumped blood into his left eye. He rode sitting on the floor in the back of the van with a wad of silk handkerchief pressed against the wound. Carmen drove point with Ski following in the truck.

The van had no side windows in back and an opaque curtain separated the prisoners from the front and the view through the windshield. Macklin's head and torso blocked the rear windows as he sat on a low kitchen chair facing front with the hand holding the magnum resting on his knee.

The two vehicles circled blocks designated earlier to throw

off the prisoners' sense of direction, went through a private parking lot, and stopped finally behind the empty building off Jefferson. An eight-foot board fence cut off the view of the river and of the Renaissance Center rearing glitteringly above the charred brick rat-infested buildings of the warehouse district. The fence had no proper gate, but Macklin and his male partners had fashioned one out of scrap lumber and an old storm door, which Ski jumped out of the truck to secure before the prisoners were allowed to alight. Ski and Deac prodded the newcomers into single file and started them toward the open back door. There Sunsmith got his first clear look at the woman standing beside it.

"Carmen?"

She said nothing. Deac grasped Sunsmith's shoulder and shoved him forward with a grunt. The Reverend stumbled, dropping his bloodied handkerchief. The cut on his forehead had dried into a blackened crust.

Macklin mounted the stairs first and stood on the landing while Sunsmith ascended, followed by the elders with Deac and Ski bringing up the rear.

"Take off that damn robe," Macklin barked.

Ski shrugged and let it slide into a heap in the dust and rat-droppings on the floor.

A third of the way up, the elder immediately behind the Reverend turned and hurled himself against the elder behind him. The column started to topple. Cursing, Deac threw a shoulder between the shoulder blades of the elder in front of him, bracing up the avalanche of bodies. The elder who had caused the trouble stared for a moment at the muzzle of Ski's automatic trained at him from the foot of the stairs, then turned around. The procession resumed.

When they were all in the hallway outside the empty dance studio, Deac strode past the three elders at the end of the line, swung his free fist low into the troublesome bodyguard's midsection, and swept the automatic hard alongside his head. The elder started to collapse. Deac grabbed the front of his shirt, popping a button, threw him up against the wall, and swept the automatic back the other way. The elder's cheek split open. Macklin watched.

Sunsmith lurched forward, stopping when Macklin's magnum came level with his own throbbing temple. "He'll kill him!"

Macklin let Deac strike the unconscious bodyguard once more, bloodying his lip. "Take him inside," he said then.

Deac held his weapon poised for another swing. Macklin had to repeat the command before he lowered it. He bettered his grip on the elder's shirt and dragged him through the open door of the studio. The injured man's heels left twin black streaks on the linoleum in the hallway.

The others followed at a prod from Ski.

Carmen had appeared atop the stairs on the end of the episode. She confronted Macklin outside the door. "Did you have to do that?"

"I didn't do anything."

"That's what I mean."

"Guns are just a prop if you don't use them."

"When I said no killing I didn't mean it was okay to turn a healthy man into a vegetable."

"He'll be all right."

"Will that man you killed last night be all right?"

"That didn't have anything to do with this."

"You bastard." Her dark face flushed. "You made me an accomplice to a murder just to protect yourself. Did you think I'd go to the police when this was finished?"

He said, "I'm not so great in bed I thought it would hold you if you got second thoughts."

She raised a hand as if to slap him. Then she lowered it. "A man's life is worth more than a roll in the hay," she said evenly.

"It's worth the going price for cartridges. In this case, though, it's worth a hundred thousand dollars." His voice was low and steady. "Don't look at me like I'm shit. You're in it for what Sunsmith fleeced you out of. Every time you pick up a gun or pay for one to be picked up you're a killer. That's what they're for. If it's for money you're a paid killer. We come from the same litter, you and I."

"Mother of God. Haven't you ever done anything for someone's life? Killing, is that the only thing you're good for?"

He stepped away from the door. "They're waiting the dance."

"Mother of God." She crossed herself and went inside.

A uniformed officer with an academy haircut peered at Pontier's badge and moved a sawhorse to let him into the alley. The inspector walked past the bullet-punched Buick and the pale limousine, almost stepping on the photographer stretched out on his back trying for a dramatic angle, and went into the building, where Sergeant Lovelady was in conversation with a gray-haired Korean he could have worn on his keychain.

"Kwan Duc, Inspector," Lovelady said. "He's Sunsmith's tailor. He heard the shots, but by the time he got up the balls to go downstairs everybody was gone."

"You always that slow, Mr. Duck?"

"Duc," the tailor corrected him. Pontier couldn't see any difference in the way he pronounced it. "I here five year. Where I from, shots come, you don't run that way."

"Your English stinks for someone who's been here that long."

"I thank." The Korean's face was smooth.

Lovelady said, "Sunsmith picked up a robe he had ordered, then left with his bodyguards. The shots came right after."

"He have an appointment?"

"He was expected."

"I don't get it. Why'd they take the bodies?"

"Maybe there weren't any. No sign of blood."

"Reverend good customer," Kwan Duc said. "Hard to fit."

Pontier scratched his moustache. "Please don't say it was a snatch."

"Not if you don't want me to."

"I go now?"

Lovelady held up an index finger. "Kwan Duc had a visitor day before yesterday. Tell the inspector."

"White elder. Strange. He want pick up Reverend's robe. Reverend he always pick up his own self."

"Would you know his face if you saw it again?" asked the inspector.

The Korean moved a shoulder.

"Show him the books. Jesus," Pontier added, "here we go again, up to our asses in reporters."

"We shouldn't of yanked Sunsmith's protection."

"We didn't, we'd have another cop funeral to go to. This was pro start to finish. Make sure he *looks* at those books."

"I got a pension says the guy ain't there."

"I wish to hell you'd quit talking about your retirement. I'm starting to think about going with you."

Outside, the photographer was trying to take a picture of his own reflection in the limousine's windshield.

CHAPTER 22

When Ski and Deac got back from ditching the van and garbage truck not far from where they had been stolen, Macklin had finished cuffing Sunsmith and his bodyguards to the brass *barre*. The manacles were a new type made of plastic as hard as steel with combination locks that thanks to employees of Hermann's had never arrived at Detroit Police Headquarters where they were intended. The blinds were drawn over the windows, and the harsh overhead light drew deep shadows in the faces of the five men sitting on the floor with their legs sprawled out in front of them and their hands raised almost in an attitude of prayer.

"Look right natural, don't they?" suggested Ski.

"My people are looking for me." Sitting with his jacket unbuttoned and salmon-colored shirt leaking from under his vest all around, great head sunk into his collar, the Reverend bore no small resemblance to a painted turtle. "You can't hold me long."

"Two hundred and twenty-five thousand dollars."

Sunsmith's head swiveled toward Carmen, standing with her back to one of the shaded windows. She had laid her MAC-10 on the ledge. She went on.

"On a conservative estimate, I figure you're worth twenty thousand per day every day you're out and about. That includes legitimate collections on top of your little investment scam. You owe me two hundred and twenty-five thousand dollars less the seed money you turned back. That's, let's see—"

"Eleven days and six hours," Deac said.

Everyone looked at him. He dipped his mohawked head in mock embarrassment. "I was studying for my CPA when I quit to join the N.A.L."

"We'll say eleven days and give you the benefit of what you returned," said Carmen. "That'll get you out on election day. Of course, it won't leave you any time to campaign against gambling."

Ski said, "I vote we don't feed him. I'll take twenty pounds in the pool."

"That's hard blubber," Deac put in. "I'll take ten."

"Watch the hallway," Macklin told Deac. "I don't want any derelicts wandering up here."

Deac went out carrying his automatic. He closed the door behind him.

Macklin said, "We'll feed him. Not what he's used to, but we're on a budget."

"Carmen, you're not a kidnapper," Sunsmith said.

"Pulling off a kidnapping makes me one. It's a lot of bother, though. I've got better things to do than babysit you and the Marx Brothers there for the next eleven days."

"Bitch." The elder with the split cheek and swollen lip got the word out muffled.

"Let us go now and we'll forget about it. Only someone's got to pay for the car your friends shot up."

"I forgot that," she said. "We'll credit it to your account. Two hours off for the car."

"I never cheated you out of a cent. I'll show you my books."

Macklin said, "Ski."

The slender black man stepped forward and twirled the combination dial on the handcuff securing the elder farthest from Sunsmith to the *barre*. The cuff sprang open. Ski stepped back. Warily the bodyguard got to his feet, the empty manacle dangling.

"That's my Carmen." Sunsmith looked expectantly at Ski, who gestured with his automatic from the elder he had freed to the door leading to the hallway. The elder walked in that direction. Ski followed him out. The door was still drifting shut when everyone in the room heard the burp. The door closed, then opened and Ski came back in alone. A thread of smoke curled out of the automatic's barrel.

"Bastards!" Fresh blood erupted from the newly opened cut on the injured elder's lip.

" 'That's my Carmen,' " mocked Carmen.

White showed around the Reverend's waxen black eyes. They closed and his chin sank farther into his collar. His lips were moving.

"What's he saying?" Macklin asked Carmen.

Her profile was taut against the sunlight leaking in around the windowshade. " 'The Lord is my shepherd.' "

" 'I shall not want,' " said Ski, grinning.

"What do you want?"

Half an hour had passed since Ski had come back into the room without the first elder. No one had spoken since Sunsmith had finished the Lord's Prayer. He was looking at the floor, and for a moment no one was sure he had spoken at all. Now the great head came up. "What do you want?"

"What do I want," Carmen said to Macklin.

"Two hundred eighteen thousand dollars," he said. "That's after taking out what he paid you back and two thousand to fix the car. I know where you can get it done for a grand."

"No, we'll be fair. I think he carries his checkbook in his left inside breast pocket."

Ski stepped forward, felt inside the Reverend's coat, and removed a slim checkbook bound in alligator covers. A gold pen was clipped to it. "What good's it?" Ski asked. "He'll just stop payment."

"No, he won't," said Macklin.

Sunsmith raised his eyes to the killer's. "I know who you are."

"The devil?"

"I should have turned your son over to the elders when I had him in my church."

"What?"

Carmen said, "Unshackle him so he can make it out."

"What about my son?" Macklin unbelted the magnum.

"I'm not making out any checks," Sunsmith said.

"Ski!"

At the command from Macklin, the black killer lifted his automatic off the window ledge and started to undo the handcuffs of the elder who was now farthest from Sunsmith. The elder cursed and tried to slide the cuff down the *barre* away from Ski, who leveled the automatic's muzzle at his face. He stopped struggling. The manacle opened.

Carmen and Macklin watched the Reverend's face as the bodyguard was pulled to his feet and propelled toward the door. The features might have belonged to a corroded idol, stony but eaten away around the eyes and mouth from wind and rain. In the hallway they heard the elder's footsteps shuffling rapidly, starting to run, terminated by a short gargling burst and then, again, the closing of the door. The elder with the battered face whimpered.

CHAPTER 23

Thursday night, Charles Maggiore, acknowledged czar of organized criminal activities throughout Detroit and its suburbs and as far south as Toledo, urinated standing up for the first time since he was shot. A one-hundred-pound blonde nurse named Mindy supported his weight with her arm around his waist and one of his arms across her shoulders and said encouraging things while he trickled into the bowl and then shook off without help. He told her he hadn't felt that proud of himself since his potty training.

Gordy was standing inside the door to the corridor when they emerged from the bathroom. In his black suit surrounded by the pastel walls and holding a bouquet of peonies he looked like Boris Karloff in the scene with the little girl in *Frankenstein*. The nurse gasped.

"It's okay, he's housebroken."

She helped the patient into bed and left, closing the door behind her.

"Shove the posies," Maggiore said. "You bring the paper?"

The big man produced a rolled-up copy of the five-star edition of the Detroit *News* from his hip pocket and lumbered forward to hand it to his employer. Maggiore unrolled it and skimmed the columns under the black headline, then demolished the first section searching for the rest of the story. Finally he shoved the whole mess into a pile on the floor.

"Fucking feds," he said. "Be like them to snatch the fat bald black bastard off a public street and make a friendly witness out of him."

"I don't think it was them."

"Well, who else would want him in cold storage?"

"I don't know, but it wouldn't make the papers if the feds done it. Not the front page, anyhow."

"Sure it would. They never tell the local cops anything. I bet that psalm-singing nigger's talking to a steno and a tape machine right now. Hanging me out to dry on that tax thing so he can walk and go right back to talking down gambling tomorrow. I never should of listened to Constable when he came to me with the deal. If I didn't need the grease to fight that gun-running rap I never would of."

"You're going to start the bleeding again you don't cool off."

"Who're you, Marcus Welby? Call Constable."

"Why don't you call him?"

"They took away my phone. Call him, tell him I got a message to send Sunsmith. What's the name of that matcher we used at the Bannerman Projects?"

"Filzer? He's a firebug. He'd touch off his sister just to see how long she burned."

"Filzer, yeah. Tell him I want Filzer. I want everything in Sunsmith's church burning but the holy water."

"What happened to not wanting to rile the voters?"

"Fuck the voters. That Bible-thumper has to be told there's

a hell here too for them that slip up. I'm through screwing with him."

Penitentiary life had hooked Michael Boniface on television for the first time in his life. He had never owned one, preferring during his few free hours to listen to his valuable collection of Italian opera records or the radio station that broadcast by satellite from Rome. But the records in Milan were all rock and strings and the Rome broadcast was after lights out, and since he had never been much for reading he had drifted into the television room, where early-evening reruns of *Daktari* and *The Patty Duke Show* quickly became his favorites. Along with a broad vocabulary of English gutter terms, this preference was the only thing he had taken with him from prison.

Marsh and Paula were trying to figure out who had let the sick leopard out of its cage when a male announcer with peroxided hair appeared on the screen announcing the abduction of the Reverend Thomas Aquinas Sunsmith from an alley downtown. Boniface stopped scratching behind Al's ears and the golden retriever raised its chin from its master's knee to look up at him.

"Picante!"

Picante came out of the bathroom zipping his fly. He glanced from his employer's tense hawklike profile to the screen, where a hand-held camera lingered on a row of bulletholes stitched across the trunk lid of a maroon-and-white Buick Electra before moving on to the empty limousine parked in front of it. The announcer's oiled baritone rolled on.

"That cocksucker Maggiore," Boniface said. "You think someone's just so stupid and then he goes and does something more stupid."

"Why didn't he just kill him?"

"Because he's so stupid he thinks he can turn him into an expressway overpass on the QT and not get blamed."

"Sweet for us. I mean, if the voters tumble and turn out in Sunsmith's favor on gambling."

"Sweet, hell. The feds and cops will shut us all down. They won't ask is this drop-spot or that whorehouse Maggiore's or Boniface's, they'll close up the town tighter than a nun's twat."

"So wait it out."

"Easy for you to say. You're not shelling out a hundred and a half a day for this suite. *Your* wife didn't divorce you and take the house while you were in prison. I got a dog and debts. I need cash I'm going to get back where I was before the world turned to shit."

"What do you want to do?"

"It's too late for Sunsmith. He's pavement by now. Blacktop, ha! We got to throw the cops a piece of meat and keep them out of the kitchen. Any luck finding Macklin?"

"I tried calling his place all day yesterday and again this morning. No answer."

"Keep trying. I hired him to deliver a package to the Wayne County Morgue that only got as far as Detroit Receiving. He's got a job to finish."

Picante lifted the receiver off the telephone. "I'm dialing."

"W.R. Fontana, Inspector. *Free Press.*"

"How are you, Bill?"

"Is Sunsmith's kidnapping connected with the attempt on his life a few weeks ago?"

"That hasn't been ruled out. So far, though, it's an abduction, not a kidnapping. There's been no ransom demand."

The rubber-faced reporter from the *Free Press* pulled his mouth into a tight grin. "We discussing semantics or is that a stall?"

"Neither. When we know something, so will you. Yes." Pontier pointed to the blonde woman in the red suit from *USA Today*.

"Is it true the police are investigating Sunsmith's finances, and if so, do you think he might have arranged his own disappearance in order to escape detection?"

"I'm a homicide inspector. You'll have to check with Fraud on that."

The fat man with a walrus moustache from Channel 4 identified himself. "What about terrorists, Inspector?"

Pontier laughed and so did most of the journalists present. That footage would make the *Eleven O'Clock News* on Channel 2 but would be edited out on 4.

"Are we to assume anything from the fact that a homicide inspector has been placed in charge of this investigation?" Fontana, the *Free Press*.

"Only that the Reverend Sunsmith has been my responsibility since the assassination attempt."

"Could this be a stunt?" put in the black man from the *News*. "Rumor has it the Reverend is planning to run for public office."

"I can't speculate on that."

"How will this affect the gambling referendum?" *USA Today*.

"Who am I, Jimmy the Greek?"

"Your answers are Greek." Fontana.

"Bill, you're a horse's ass."

The man from the *News* grinned. "Well, there goes TV."

"Inspector!"

"Inspector!"

The press conference continued for another minute, ending abruptly when a scruffy-bearded, bespectacled young writer representing *Monthly Detroit* asked Pontier if he would feel comfortable wearing stripes with plaid. The inspector went back upstairs to the Criminal Investigation Division while a pair of uniformed officers ushered the reporters out to the front steps of 1300. Lovelady followed him.

"Where'd that bitch hear about Sunsmith's finances?" Pontier demanded.

"This place has more leaks than a lace firehose."

"See what you can do about stopping some of them up."

"You want I should tap the phones?"

"I don't care if you have to wire the bitch's panties. I can't work in a glass bowl."

The sergeant was wheezing from the climb. "I should of put in when I had my twenty."

"How's Duck?"

They had entered the squad room. Lovelady, out of breath, inclined his head toward the gray-haired Korean sitting at the sergeant's desk with a stack of mug books at his elbow and another spread open in front of him.

"That's not the same book."

"It's the same page."

"That mean anything?"

"Maybe not. His record so far is fifteen minutes." Lovelady mopped his face with a handkerchief.

"What's he doing, fitting them for suits?"

"Want me to goose him?"

"Not just yet." The inspector went into his office trailing the sergeant and started opening and closing drawers in his desk, shuffling through the contents. Finally he lifted out a bundle of manila interdepartmental envelopes bound together with a wide rubber band and thrust it at Lovelady. "Have him go through these when he's done with that book. They're readers and some wire photos of some scroats we haven't got our loop around yet."

"Constitutional question."

"No cop ever lost his job for making a bust that didn't stick in court. Plenty of them have over things like dead famous black ministers who could've been saved by bending the Bill of Rights a little. If he sees the man who came around asking about Sunsmith's robe in there, holler."

"I'll have him look. Maybe we'll be out of here by sunup."

The sergeant went out, carrying the bundle.

When he came back in forty-five minutes later, his eyes were glittering.

CHAPTER 24

At age ten, Carmen Contrale had helped stock her family's larder selling maps to buried pirate treasure and locks of Henry Morgan's hair with her brother Francisco to fishermen and vacationers visiting from the States. She hadn't seen Francisco since her wedding to Martin Thalberg and when last heard from he was a major in the Marxist revolutionary army in charge of procuring grubs from trees for the company mess.

At seventeen she was taking off her clothes to music in the coastal nightspots outside Managua and taking them off to no music and better money in the rooms upstairs. By then she was married to a man named Paulo Minuto, the owner of a boat and a sign reading PAULO'S CHARTER SERVICE, but known as the Minuteman in the islands, where he made deliveries under cover of darkness twice weekly until his body washed ashore at Port-au-Prince during high shark season with its lower half missing. She worked the streets for a while after that, and then a photographer scouting beach locations for a Chicago-based travel agency brochure happened to snap her picture and two weeks later she found herself in a white bikini walking down a deserted stretch of beach in Costa Rica on the arm of a homosexual weightlifter named Crew. She was paid five hundred dollars for posing.

The picture the agency selected found its way onto billboards and a full-page ad in a national magazine, after which she was offered a contract by a modeling agency headquartered in San Francisco. She never saw California or met the man who countersigned the contract, but for five years she posed against Central American sunsets in varying stages of undress and all oiled up in pink yarn bikinis trying not to slide off the waxed hoods of new automobiles parked on Guatemalan beaches and in the jungles of Belize. The contract was not renewed—she was coming on twenty-six, after all, and the crooked strip of land discovered by Balboa was acrawl with nubile post-pubescents who photographed well—but by that time she had a half-interest in an airline shuttle service consisting of a twin-engine Cessna and a pilot partner named Hector, who wore a pencil moustache and a silk scarf like Smilin' Jack and made love like Harry Reems.

They had been in business almost three years when the pilot was arrested by the United States Border Patrol in Nogales for transporting Mexican nationals into the U.S. without visas. He was given probation and released, but the plane was confiscated and the Honduran Government secured a restraining order preventing the company access to its funds. The partnership was dissolved.

Carmen was employed as a hostess in a hotel restaurant in Port Barrios when she met and seated a big red-faced *norteamericano* named Thalberg, a wealthy young industrialist addicted to safari coats and the legend of Michael Rockefeller. He was attracted to the woman's dark complexion and light hair and asked her to join him for dinner. When she demurred, explaining that she would lose her job, he asked to speak to the manager. Following a short, whispered conversation, the manager himself seated her. In the days that came after, Carmen found herself swept up into a world where the same gold card that got them through the doors of white houses in the hills where latinos in dinner jackets raked in stacks of chips with ivory scrapers was also good in dark, fish-smelling huts on the harbor where señoritas of indefinite breeding performed acts more basic. At the end of a week the couple were married in Trujillo.

At thirty-three she had become a widow for the second time, having identified and buried the swollen thing tipped into the Arno by Florentine kidnappers, and the heiress to seven million dollars in cash and securities and an additional nine million tied up in offshore oil interests, the automobile industry, and genetic research. In twenty-six years she had come from the back-street tattoo emporiums and scent shops where a *turista* with funds and the proper references could secure women and white powder to a big house and four professionally kept acres in Bloomfield Hills. But she felt that she had grown up only within the past twenty-four hours.

In that time, she had become an accessory to kidnapping and murder, dictated an extortion demand, and watched a man in whose fundamental piety she had held faith despite his ambition and greed sit motionless while three of his own followers went to their executions because he wouldn't sign a check for two hundred and eighteen thousand dollars. She had written off the first elder, supposing that Sunsmith would suspect a bluff until he heard the report of the machine gun and saw Ski return to the dance studio alone. She had thought that the threat of killing a second bodyguard would crack him. But he had let Ski lead the man out and had still not moved or spoken when the third elder, he of the cut cheek and puffed lip, was dragged, struggling and cursing and wetting his pants, by Macklin and Ski together into the hallway.

There are no holy men, she thought. Not one.

The Reverend said, "Give me the book."

Carmen took a second to react, his voice was so low. By

the time she called to Ski to hold his fire, her words were drowned out by the burst.

The bald head came down.

Macklin and Ski came back in as Carmen was unlocking Sunsmith's handcuffs. For several moments after his arm came free he sat with his hands hanging inside his thighs, still looking at the floor. Carmen had been holding the checkbook and pen in front of him for a few seconds before he raised his eyes and then his hands to accept the items. Macklin stepped forward and gripped the hand holding the pen.

"What about my son?"

He had to say it again, staring down into the black candle-dripping eyes, before the Reverend showed understanding. A pale tongue moved over his lips with a sound like fine sandpaper moving over smooth wood. "He came to me last Sunday looking for a job. I knew who he was. I sent him away."

"Was he there to kill you?"

"I don't know. I can't think of another reason."

"Maybe he found God." Ski was grinning.

"What did he say?"

"He said he wanted to get straight."

Macklin waited. "That's all?"

"That's what it came to. He left of his own will."

He let go of Sunsmith's hand. Carmen said, "Just sign your name. We'll fill in the rest."

"You stop payment we burn you," Ski said. "Your security's a fucking joke."

"He knows all that," said Macklin. He waited while Sunsmith finished signing, then seized the book, tore out the check, handed it to Carmen, and tossed the book into the Reverend's lap. "Spring the bodyguard."

Ski spun the dial of the lock securing the manacle to the last elder's wrist. The big man in blue got up, stumbling when his knee threatened to give out. Ski, all wiry muscle encased in a slender frame, took Sunsmith's hand and heaved him to his feet with a backward-leaning lunge. The checkbook slid to the floor. Changing hands on the automatic, Ski bent to pick it up.

The elder lurched forward, clawing with both hands for the pistol in Ski's off hand. Ski swung it around, pressing the trigger.

"No!" Carmen grabbed at the killer's arm. The first bullet out of the muzzle struck the elder's wrist, making him gasp. The rest slapped the wall behind him, chewing paint and filling the room with the stench of spent powder and burnt cork. When it was over the elder stood holding his wrist with threads of blood hanging between his fingers.

When Macklin was sure the shooting was over he handed his magnum to Carmen and stepped forward to pull the bodyguard's hand away from the wound. He reached inside the elder's coat, withdrew a handkerchief, twirled it into a braid, and knotted it tightly around the man's forearm above the hole. "The bullet's still in there. Get to an emergency clinic."

The prisoners shuffled swayingly toward the door, the elder cradling his tourniqueted arm. The Reverend appeared unaware of what had just happened. He moved like an old man who had lost his room in a nursing home. With a flourish, Ski grasped the knob and swung the door open, revealing Deac crouched on a high stool in the hallway with the other three elders lying face down on the floor with their hands cuffed behind their backs, their heads craning around to look at the newcomers. The floor was a litter of empty shell casings and plaster dust dislodged from the bullet-tattered ceiling.

"Foooled you," Ski sang, showing teeth.

The air in Macklin's Southfield home smelled like bad breath. After unlocking the front door he left it open for draft and went upstairs to lock the magnum away in the safe in his file cabinet. Having it away from his person and out of sight was a relief. The only time he didn't feel uneasy carrying a weapon was when he was using it; the rest of the time it rode inside his belt waiting to get him arrested. It was his usual practice once an assignment was completed to get rid of the gun immediately, and although he had disposed of the slug that had killed Hank and this piece was to all intents and purposes virgin, he had planned to dump it as well. But that was before he had learned his son was mixed up with the Reverend Sunsmith.

The revolver put away, he went back downstairs, closed the front door, and turned into the kitchen to fix himself a meal.

He had known killers who drank after a job, and even a few who used drugs to come down from the dizzy adrenalin high that only killing another human being could create, although those who employed them eroded their judgment and either got themselves killed working or became the sort of liability that they were paid to eliminate. Macklin ate. He was neither a gourmet nor a glutton, and in truth didn't think much about food one way or the other. But he abstained from food when working so that the blood and oxygen meant for his brain wouldn't have to detour through his stomach, and at 11:45 P.M. on this particular working Thursday he had not ingested anything but water since Wednesday morning. He made four slices of toast, placed two slices of processed American cheese between each pair, and let them grill in the microwave oven he had gotten from his ex-wife in the settlement while he filled a glass with milk.

Eating, he felt his blood slowing and the electricity level going down. His memory kicked in then. After they had turned loose the Reverend and his elders, Ski and Deac had raced through the dance studio with handkerchiefs, eradicating their fingerprints from everything they had conceivably touched, Ski muttering that if they had just gone ahead and killed the hostages they would have saved themselves the trouble. But Carmen reminded him that no bank would have honored Sunsmith's check in the event of his death or mysterious disappearance. Deac had suggested they torch the place. Macklin said that making arson look like anything other than arson for the benefit of the insurance company was not one of his talents and that Hermann had too much tied up in the building to take a dead loss, did Deac want to wake up on the floor of the Detroit River with a fish staring at him? He didn't say that there was no real point even in removing the evidence of their presence, since Sunsmith wasn't about to invite a probe into his finances by swearing out a complaint against them for kidnapping and extortion. And he would make it worth the elders' while, especially the wounded one's, to forget the incident as well, depend on that. Macklin didn't say these things, because he didn't want Ski and Deac to get into the habit of ignoring caution, and he might want to work with them again.

Not that he'd have to. As they were leaving, Carmen handed each of the three men a key to a safety deposit box belonging to a different bank. Macklin's share would come to eighty thousand dollars.

He wasn't thinking about the money, however. He remembered how straight Carmen's back was under the green jumpsuit as she walked through the open gate behind the empty building, separately from the others as agreed. She hadn't looked back at Macklin, standing at the back door holding the box containing the abandoned weapons, who watched her go.

It had been a short walk to the river, where he dumped the guns into the water, then tossed the empty box toward the middle to darken and grow soggy and eventually sink to the bottom among the Coke bottles, ring tabs, used prophylactics, and gnawed human bones submerged downstream. He caught a cab on Lafayette and took it to the west side parking garage where he had left the Camaro. Then home.

Such actions after all these years were automatic, requiring little thought and scarcely remembered. This could be a danger, he knew, like becoming so familiar with a heavy machine that one lost respect for its ability to crush and tear and amputate living limbs. But Macklin was still seeing Carmen's straight back when the telephone hooked to a separate line that went only into his study started ringing.

The interior light in the Camaro sprang on in the cool morning shade, then off as the driver's door was pulled shut and the engine growled into life. The two men sitting in the front seat of the white Oldsmobile parked across the street slid down when it turned out of the driveway into traffic. They started up and followed, executing a U-turn behind a Mayflower van.

The passenger unhooked the microphone from the Oldsmobile's dash. "Twelve in, over."

"Headquarters, twelve," crackled a voice from the speaker. "What's your twenty?"

"Beech Road between Eleven and Twelve. Suspect is moving, should we take him?"

"Negative, twelve. Instructions are to follow and report, over."

"We hear you. Twelve out." The passenger, a reedy redhead on temporary plainclothes assignment from Traffic, peered through the windshield at the low green car sliding along the center line. "Nice wheels."

The driver snorted. He was black, with a gray moustache cradled in the curve of an underslung lower lip. Three years on Homicide, five on Vice, seven on Missing Persons, four in uniform busting heads down Gratiot. "Them sports jobs kill you for gas and insurance. Car's just to get you there from here. It ain't a house or a woman."

The redhead wasn't listening. "These snuff guys sure take care of themselves."

CHAPTER 25

"Look at that big grayback. Who's he remind you of?"

Picante joined his employer at the railing to look down at the polar bears in the pit. The smaller of the two biggest males, buttermilk-colored with a broad silver streak down its back, sat on one of the big rocks watching the cubs swimming, their eyes closed against the spray, whiskers drooping, paddling like dogs but much faster. The bear's great paws rested on its swollen belly.

"Bert Lahr."

"Naw. Closer to home. C'mon, who?" Boniface freed a peanut skin from between his teeth with the end of his little finger and reached into the bag for another peanut.

Picante squinted, then drew his upper lip back from his long upper teeth. "Nicky Bazooka."

"Right. Same big gut. He was all the time rubbing it and patting it, like he was expecting any day."

"Jesus, I haven't thought about him in years."

"What was it, dynamite?"

"No. Hell, no. I just walked around his lock while he was out and replaced the light switch inside the door with a circuit breaker and blew out the pilot light on his stove. Place was full of gas when he got in and flipped the switch. They peeled his face off the far wall of the apartment next door."

"Poor old Nicky."

"Poor old Nicky," Picante agreed. "I was engaged to his daughter once."

"There he is."

Macklin was coming down the footpath along the iron railing. The sky was overcast, threatening rain, and he and the two men waiting for him were the only people in sight in that part of the Detroit Zoo. He had on a corduroy sportcoat and khaki trousers. When he drew within speaking distance he said: "You're early."

"I'm a suspicious old greaseball," said Boniface. "I say nine o'clock, I know you'll be here at eight, so I come at seven. If I had the brains to wipe my ass I'd set my watch ahead two hours and be done with it. How are you?"

"What do you want to talk about?"

Picante was holding a copy of the morning *Free Press*. He unrolled it and held it out in both hands. The headline read: SUNSMITH RELEASED UNHARMED.

"I heard," Macklin said. "Good news. Dead clergymen are hell on business."

"Look below the fold." Boniface sounded impatient.

A square piece in the lower right-hand corner of the front page detailed Charles Maggiore's continued recovery from his bullet wounds. It was accompanied by a recent photograph of a healthy Maggiore taken at his arraignment in federal court on the gun-running charge.

"Nice picture."

"Where's the black border?" Picante refolded the paper.

"I put two where his heart should be. How'd I know he didn't have one?"

Boniface said, "A miss is a miss. Happens. But it's been

almost two weeks and there he is taking up bedspace when there's empty slabs at the morgue."

"There's no percentage in planning a hit in a hospital. You've got the police to worry about on top of the security staff, and even if you get around them you never know who's going to be coming down the hall when you drop the hammer, maybe an off-duty cop or just a Sunday hero. Too many variables."

"I took out a bookkeeper on the fourth floor of Detroit General eight years ago," Picante said blandly.

"Then the job's yours."

"I told you that's past. Maybe if everyone else was shooting at the same fish."

Boniface spat out a bad peanut. The polar bear that looked like Nicky Bazooka turned albino-pink eyes on him from its rock. "When you fixing to take him?"

Macklin said, "I'm not."

"I mean after he gets out of the hospital."

"Not then either. I'm walking away from this one."

"Shit. He's holding you up for more cash, Mike. Guy blows the hit the first time and now he wants a raise."

Boniface told Picante to shut up. He was looking at Macklin with eyes grown less clear and piercing in prison. "I named a figure and you said okay. That was always as much contract as we needed. Okay, the world's changed. What's the tariff?"

"Five hundred thousand."

"Five hun- . . . Half a million *dollars?*"

"A million."

Picante said shit.

"Two million," Macklin said. "Pick a figure, I won't take it. Get yourself another button."

"This is Carlo Maggiore we're talking about, the one hired a soldier to take you out two years ago. The guy that turned your own kid into a killer just because he knew it would tear your heart out. You don't want to hit *him?*"

"I don't feel anything about him anymore. He's meat for the feds now. They can have him."

"This ain't Macklin talking. Macklin wouldn't leave a job unfinished."

"You mean he wouldn't walk out on twenty thousand," Picante said. "Unless he got a better offer."

Macklin said, "Some advice, Mike. Drop this guy before he heels over and pulls you down on top of him. He thinks too much for a gofer."

Boniface looked sad. "Just because a man's in the can don't mean he can't still see through walls. I know most of that hundred grand I gave you year before last went for the house the judge gave your wife in the settlement. You can't live on what's left and you're too old to learn meat-cutting by mail. You turn loose of this job, you won't get the contract on a sick goldfish."

"Don't worry about me."

"I can't help it. Sometimes when I look at you I see that skinny punk hanging around Hermann's junkyard waiting for his old man to show."

"I was a fat kid, Mike. And the closest you ever got to Hermann's junkyard was the guy you sent to watch and make sure the right stiffs got ground up in the crusher. You're the finger and I'm the trigger. Don't try to make anything more out of it than that."

"I got to ask where your living's coming from if not from me." There was now no trace of softness in the older man's heavy features.

Picante said, "Watch your blood pressure, Mike. I'll talk to him."

The pair started walking.

"You got to be careful what you say to these old moustache petes," said Picante. "That Roman blood goes straight up their ass. It's like Caesar never died and the last couple of thousand years didn't happen."

"Only since prison. He didn't used to be like that." Macklin's eyes were on the ape house straight ahead.

"A lot of things ain't like they were when he went in. He wants to turn the clock back. It ain't healthy. I don't think old Mike's going to be with us much longer."

Macklin said nothing.

"Take Maggiore," Picante went on. "In the old days we'd just pop him and all our problems would be over. It ain't that simple now. Christ, he delegates so much his fucking office boy could run things if he swallowed the pill tomorrow. We could blow down his whole organization, but then the papers and TV would start screaming massacre and we'd all wind up getting run bare-assed out of town. No, these days you've got to be more indirect.

"Mike wants to put down Maggiore and get his ass back into the driver's seat, but he wants to do it before Maggiore puts down Sunsmith or he's afraid there won't be a driver's seat to get his ass back into. That's the old way of thinking. As I see it nowadays, kill a crook, kill a reverend, you get the same amount of heat either way, especially after the public finds out some of the things Sunsmith was into at the time he met his well-deserved fate. A story like that takes time to sink in, so allow for a week or so of heavy shit. Meanwhile the gambling referendum gets voted out because the good holy man died in the cause of God. In the long run the heat's down and so's gambling, and guess who's in the driver's seat then."

"Carmine Picante," Macklin said.

They had stopped outside the ape house. Shrugging exaggeratedly, Picante thrust his bony hands into his pants pockets. "Well, someone other than Maggiore. What can you do to hurt narcotics, make them legal? Not likely. Okay, you don't want to do Maggiore. Maybe you'll give the Reverend a thought. How'd you like the slot machine franchise in Iroquois Heights? Pays about half a mill, before and after taxes."

"Will you pay it to my estate after Sunsmith's bodyguards finish cutting me down?"

"Fuck the bodyguards. Four guys just did without even spilling any blood hardly. Hey, maybe you know them. The thing had style."

"I haven't been following it."

"I bet it was them Criselli brothers out of Farmington Hills. Them cowboys would rape the mayor's daughter if he had one and send him a bill for the stud fee. Or, hell, maybe it wasn't a kidnapping at all. That story Sunsmith told about masked men and being held in a dark room and then dumped downtown from a van at midnight sounds like bullshit. Maybe it bought him a few hundred votes."

"Maybe."

Picante shrugged again. "You want to think about the offer, get back to me?"

"I thought about it."

"Sure?"

Macklin nodded.

Picante nodded too. His long face lengthened. "I guess you're just as much into the old way of doing things as Mike. It's a good thing your son ain't."

He returned to the polar bear pit, leaving Macklin standing there.

The white Oldsmobile was parked on the other side of the children's petting zoo with a view through the bars of the ape house and the man standing near it and the other returning to the third man leaning on the railing over the pit. The redheaded officer lowered his binoculars and handed them to his partner behind the wheel. "You make the guy in the cheap suit?"

The black detective focused the binoculars, turning the wheel again as he slid them from the long-faced man in baggy polyester to the man in the corduroy coat and back to the heavy man eating peanuts. "Don't have to." He laid them on the seat. "Guy looking at the bears is Mike Boniface."

"Who he?"

"Before your time, like damn near everything else. Keep your eyes on Macklin." He radioed headquarters.

CHAPTER 26

FLIM-FLAM FAKER
THE GEEKS
METRONOME RECORDS
OCTOBER 1972

Reading the inscription in the brass plate screwed to the plaque in Sunsmith's office, Inspector Pontier wasn't sure if he remembered the tune or not. Every time he tried humming it to himself it came out *The Flatfoot Floosie with the Floy-Floy.* Floy-doy, floy-doy. He wondered what would come out if you took down the gold record and tried to play it. Didn't matter. He was only looking at the thing because the twice-life-size portrait behind the desk of Sunsmith in Day-Glo made his eyes swim.

Looking at the Reverend in the flesh was no comfort. He was seated at the altar-shaped desk in lavender shirtsleeves and maroon vest with a gold stripe and a gold silk necktie tucked into the V. Despite his drawn appearance and lack of luster in his black eyes, he made Sergeant Lovelady, sitting across from him in the visitor's chair, seem quiet in his yellow sportcoat.

Nobody was talking at the moment. Sunsmith's letter opener, slim silver with a handle fashioned after St. Christopher, made sibilant sounds as he slit one envelope after another, laying each aside without removing its contents to reach for the next. The corners of paper currency poked out of several of those he had opened.

"It stinks, Your Holiness." Pontier turned away from the gold record. "Nobody snatches a prominent clergyman and his four bodyguards off a public street in broad daylight and holds them for thirty-two hours just to let them go."

"You've spoken to the elders." Sunsmith went on slitting envelopes.

"You over-rehearsed them. Same words, pauses all in the same places, even the one in the hospital had it down cold. They should put together a brother act, sing *a cappella.*"

"How *is* Brother Julian?"

"They're holding him for observation at Receiving in case of infection. The inside of his coatsleeve was the only thing that kept the bullet from passing straight through his wrist, the doc said. Those steel-jacketed jobs are like grease through a goose. Only things smoother are the lies he told us."

"You overestimate my authority, Inspector." Slit, slit. "Two of the elders handed in their resignations this morning. I expect Brother Julian to do the same when he's released."

"I bet the severance pay is sweet." This was Lovelady.

Slit, slit.

Pontier said, "Know what I think? I think Mike Boniface had you taken, figuring everyone would blame Charles Maggiore and come out against gambling in the referendum Tuesday a week. That's what I think."

"If that's true it was kind of him to let me go." Slit, slit.

"I'm still working on that part. Meanwhile Lovelady has another theory. Tell him, Sergeant."

"Maggiore wouldn't chance killing you," Lovelady said, folding his hands across his middle. "But if your story holds any water at all, it could be he took you and then let you go so you could tell it and nobody would believe you. Discredit you with the grass roots."

The letter opener paused. "Like Aimee Semple McPherson."

"The thing's got stunt written all over it," said Pontier. "Which is another theory."

"A man was shot." Sunsmith slit the final three envelopes and shuffled the lot into a neat stack in front of him. Then he laid his palms flat on the blotter. His gaze met the inspector's.

"In the wrist, missing everything vital. Some men might consider it worth a bonus." He went on before the Reverend could interrupt. "I don't think it was a stunt. If it was you'd have a better story, a daring escape under cover of darkness, one of your men was shot, you gave him your shoulder during the breathless dash to safety, that shit. Not a gimmick, then. Maybe a disgruntled investor."

"I like that one too," said Lovelady.

"We kicked it around. Just for now, though, we're going by the book, and the first rule in investigative theory is to keep it simple. From the start Boniface's stood the most to gain from your death. He pulled the string on that hophead who tried to ice you two weeks ago and when that didn't work he decided to be more subtle and had you snatched. Maybe your body was supposed to show up in the trunk of a stolen car at Metro Airport, or maybe he was just fixing to keep you under wraps until after the referendum and let everyone think the worst. Either way the measure would go down along with Maggiore's hopes and Boniface would come in and scoop up the leavings. I don't know what went wrong.

My guess is you bought off the thugs he had babysitting you. There's no honor left among thieves if there ever was any to begin with."

"Are you arresting me?"

"What for? There's no law against lying to a police officer, much as we need one. Anyway, I'm not in a mood to play King Herod today. The sergeant there has a pension to think about and I've still got eleven years to go on my thirty. No, I'm just letting you know it stinks and that I'm going to be coming around sniffing to see if it goes away or it gets worse. What's that about the bird's fall?"

"The sparrow." Sunsmith stroked his thumb over the letter opener's smooth surface, clouding it. "He marks the sparrow's fall."

"Yeah. Well, so long, sparrow."

Lovelady rose. The two detectives were at the door when Sunsmith's telephone rang. They paused while the Reverend answered it. He held out the receiver. "You gave your people this number?"

"I knew you wouldn't mind." Pontier came over and accepted it. "Pontier. Okay. He make him positive? Uh-huh, he still following Macklin? No, that's what I wanted, I know where to find the big man. Okay." He hung up. To Lovelady: "Leonard and Hurst called in from the zoo. Macklin just made contact with Mike Boniface."

The sergeant's pockmarked features barely stirred. "Just once before I retire I'd like to be right."

"We ought to both order suits from that Korean just to thank him for IDing Macklin."

"Speak for yourself. There's five years' more wear in this coat."

The pair left. After the door closed, Sunsmith used the letter opener to cut the blotter to shreds.

CHAPTER 27

At forty, evidence of simple absentmindedness—misplacing things, overlooking details once routine—were like the first chill of one's own mortality. When one killed for a living they were a double whammy.

When Macklin glanced up at his rearview mirror on his way home and spotted the white Oldsmobile rounding the corner behind him, he couldn't say that he had actually *seen* the car parked in the zoo or following him there, but he knew that it had been in both places. Younger and less complacent, he'd have spied the tail earlier and thrown it off before meeting Boniface. Now he knew the empty-bucket feeling inside of a boy caught masturbating.

Belatedly, automatically, he let the speedometer slacken to twenty climbing a hill on Ten Mile Road, noting with satisfaction that the driver of the Oldsmobile followed suit when the gap began to close. He waited until he had drifted over the crest, then flattened the accelerator pedal. The Camaro's big engine hesitated, gulping, then shot forward with a squeal of smoking rubber. He took a curve on the outside where the road banked, narrowly missing a Jeep Wagoneer coming in his direction when he switched lanes, whisked through the red light at Southfield Road during the pause following the change, struck sparks off the pavement when he bottomed out at the base of the next hill, and swung north on Evergreen on the yellow. There he slowed down. He hadn't seen the Oldsmobile since the first hill.

After turning a few corners to make sure he had lost it, he took the John Lodge south to Carmen Thalberg's bank. The safety deposit key was burning a hole in his pocket and a man in hiding from the police needed cash.

"That fucking salt-and-pepper team lost Macklin," Lovelady reported.

Pontier's shoulders slumped. He was standing at his office bulletin board, which he had stripped in order to pin up photographs of the Reverend Sunsmith and Michael Boniface's mug shot and the FBI wire photo of Peter Macklin that the Korean tailor had identified as a picture of the man who had come in asking about Sunsmith. Lovelady recognized the procedure as a sign that his superior had determined not to leave the room until he had solved the puzzle. He would mix and match the pictures, change their order, discard some, and maybe add others until a pattern began to show. When the fever was on him it reminded the sergeant of Red Skelton's Freddie the Freeloader constructing a tuxedo and top hat out of rags, soot, chalk, and tar paper. What he wound up with might not always be the real thing, but it was almost always close enough to pass.

The pause was short. Then the inspector selected a shot of Charles Maggiore inside the lobby of the Frank Murphy Hall of Justice and made room for it between Macklin and Boniface. He stood looking at the tableau for a second, then shook his head and took down Maggiore. " 'Kay, flag an APB on Macklin and a BOL on his car. General Service should have his license number on file."

"Armed and dangerous?"

Pontier glanced back over his shoulder. "You want to fuck with him?"

"A and D," Lovelady agreed. "Anything else?"

"Yeah, pick up Boniface and anyone who's with him."

"Warrant?"

"Questioning."

When the sergeant had left, Pontier unpinned Boniface's picture and tried it next to Macklin's, then put Maggiore's on the other side of the killer's. He stepped back to look at it. After a moment he turned to his desk and shuffled through the contents of the thick file on the Sunsmith case spread out there. He skimmed through the reports, parts of which he knew by heart. His eye caught on the one filed by Officer Paul Ledyard. He read it through twice, then examined the material clipped to it. This included a photocopy from the department's own microfilmed newspaper files of a long Sunday supplement piece on a tall, tawny-haired woman pictured crossing a street in Miami. She had on khaki shorts that left her long legs bare and a flowered print shirt with the tails tied under her breasts and she was turning her head toward the camera, a finger pushing down her sunglasses so she could see who was taking her picture. She had dark eyes.

Not all of the article was included in the photocopy. He had ordered it just for the picture, to help identify her for the officer he had sent to pick her up for questioning. He read what was there, then detached it from the report and unpinned Maggiore and pinned the article and picture in its place next to Macklin. His heart was starting to thud. Without pausing he moved an old publicity mug of the Reverend Sunsmith taken during his show business days into the space on the other side of the woman. He didn't know until he saw the blood that he'd stuck one of his fingers with the pin.

Sucking the digit, he swept the debris off the telephone on

his desk and punched a button. The line buzzed several times.

"Records." A woman's voice, sleepy.

"Where the hell were you?"

"The shift is changing. I just came on."

"What, is the clutch stuck?"

"Huh?"

"This is Inspector Pontier. Send me up everything in the newspaper file on Carmen Contrale Thalberg. That's Carmen common Charlie Only Nebraska Tennessee Rudolph . . ." He lost his place. "Screw it, I'll come down and get it myself." He threw the receiver at the cradle, hurrying.

CHAPTER 28

She wasn't escorted into an office this time. It was a small room painted beige with no windows and a table and chairs and a bare overhead bulb closed off in a cage. She asked the officer, a young black man in uniform, if she should be calling her lawyer. He said that was up to her and that if she wanted to he'd tell the inspector. She said, "Not yet." He went out and closed the door on her.

No one brought coffee. Ten minutes passed. She was starting to feel claustrophobic for the first time in her life when Inspector Pontier entered. He was wearing a camel's-hair jacket and a brown knitted tie on a champagne-colored shirt. His gray eyes were light in his dark face. He sat down opposite her and said, "Is there anything you want to tell me?"

She laughed. "You sound like Judge Hardy."

"Where'd you meet Macklin?"

She let the merriment fade slowly from her face. "Who's Macklin?"

"My guess would be right here at thirteen hundred. He came in on a sweep the same day I asked you about your business with Sunsmith. Someone will remember."

"I don't know what you want me to say."

He sat back, looking at her. She had on a gray silk blazer over a red top. Gray shirt, red shoes. The purse on the table was red leather. "A girl grows up on the streets of Central America fleecing tourists with her brother within earshot of Marxist guerrilla gunfire. She becomes an entertainer, which down there means she hooks a little on the side when she isn't performing with spider monkeys onstage. She hangs around with smugglers, one of whom is her first husband, who gets himself fed to the fish for fucking with the Colombians, excuse my French. Long before she falls into money she's learned to play up to the wrong element to survive. Hell, maybe she even knew the scroats who popped her second husband and made a rich widow out of her. Maybe she set it up."

"That's bullshit and you know it!" She reached for her purse. His hand shot out and closed around her wrist.

"That part maybe." His voice remained even. "The rest is all there in the white spaces between the lines of everything that's ever been written about you. Change the setting to Detroit and every third hooker on Michigan Avenue will tell the same story. You show a long history of poor judgment in your choice of friends, señorita."

His grip was cutting off her circulation. She glared, not showing it. "Am I under arrest?"

"No. If we tried booking you now you'd be out so fast your shoes would be smoking." He let go. "It's no fun being smarter than the entire criminal justice system. I know you hired Macklin and some others to take Sunsmith and throw the fear of God into him, so to speak. No one who started out shucking and jiving the anglos takes to getting shucked and jived herself, particularly when it's up in the numbers you famous rich folk like to roll in. But the court's from Missouri;

it says show me. Maybe you even got some of those numbers back, although that wouldn't be as important as letting the good Reverend know he can't shit a shitter."

"I assume I can go." She put both hands on her purse.

"I didn't want to give up on Boniface. When I figured out that he or his people were behind the attempt on Sunsmith, and especially after Sunsmith was kidnapped and released and then Macklin was seen meeting with Boniface at the zoo, I was stone sold on him. But he wouldn't snatch Sunsmith just to let him go, and Sunsmith wouldn't buy off Macklin. That's why Macklin's reached the age he has in his business. He always goes home with the one who brought him to the dance. I thought about Sunsmith's disgruntled investors, and for a minute or so Charles Maggiore looked good. Then he didn't, for the same reason I ruled him out in the try in the church two weeks ago. He stands a lot more to lose from a dead or a kidnapped Sunsmith than he does from a live one at the pulpit. All of the other investors were businessmen, and about as respectable as you can expect businessmen to be these days. Except one."

"I really am leaving."

"Not all of the minority stereotypes are wrong," he said. "My Uncle Jonas was a pretty good tap dancer on the Chataqua Circuit, and every month or so I get a real craving for barbecued ribs, just have to have 'em. And you've got the Latin temper. When someone screws you, you screw them back twice as hard. You shouldn't have shot that bodyguard. He didn't have anything to do with Sunsmith's scam."

"*I* didn't—" She closed her mouth. Then she rose, clutching her purse. "I'll catch a cab home. Don't trouble yourself."

Pontier made as if to get up, then swept out an arm and snatched the purse from her grip. She lunged for it, but he clapped it to his stomach and tilted his chair back out of her reach. "Rich people hardly ever carry cash. I've been wondering what it is about this purse that you won't take your hands off it." He opened the clasp.

"That's illegal search and seizure!" A flush stained her tawny features.

He rummaged through the contents of the purse and came up with a folded rectangle of paper, which he snapped open one-handed. His expression didn't change as he looked at it. He returned it to the interior and snapped shut the clasp. "The Shadow was wrong," he said, holding out the purse. "It pays."

She hesitated before accepting the purse. "My business dealings with the Reverend don't concern the police."

"Give me some credit, Mrs. Thalberg." He sounded tired. "Without someone to sign a complaint there's no kidnapping. I can't arrest you for carrying around a check for an obscene amount of money. But don't let's pretend I just fell off the potato wagon. Spare me that much."

"May I go?"

"I wish to hell you would."

She tipped the cab driver five dollars and walked up the flagged path without looking back as he turned around in the driveway. On the porch she opened her purse, then remembered she had left her keys inside. She rang the bell.

Elizabeth was a long time coming to the door. The black maid unlocked and opened it enough to see Carmen, then undid the chain and swung it wide. Her face was taut.

Carmen said, "I hope you haven't started dinner. I'm not hungry."

"I'll eat it."

She jumped and turned toward the dining room arch. Macklin came through it, holding the magnum without pointing it. Light reflected flatly off its mirror surface. He said, "I need a place to stay. The cops will be waiting for me at my house."

"There are motels." Her voice was toneless.

"They'll be all over them. I was parked across the street

when they came for you. I figure they won't be back here for a while."

"Pontier saw the check. I was on my way out to cash it when they came. If they find out you're here they'll arrest both of us."

"We'll have to make sure they don't find out." He glanced at the maid.

"Don't worry about Elizabeth," Carmen said. "Her green card depends on this job."

"I never worry about anything." He belted the revolver. "What's for dinner?"

"I must be crazy."

Moonlight tented the furniture in the master bedroom and lay pale on the sheet against Carmen's dark skin. She lay close to Macklin, not cuddling. He said, "You're not crazy."

"You call it, then. I'm too old to still be attracted to bad men."

"It's got nothing to do with age."

"How does a man get to be a killer?"

"You mean what's a nice boy like me doing in a business like this?"

"You're not a nice boy."

"Some of us marry sixteen million dollars. The rest of us do what we're good at to get along."

She propped herself up on one elbow to look at him. The sheet fell, exposing one breast. "Maybe marrying sixteen million dollars is what some of us are good at. You're kind of moralistic for an assassin."

He said nothing.

"I never asked you if you were married," she said. "Are you?"

His grin was wolfish in the pale light. "You're worried about adultery?"

"I just like to know a little something about the men I sleep with. Are you married?"

"Not now."

"Children?"

"One boy." The grin had vanished.

"How old?"

"Let's go to sleep."

He turned his back to her. She snaked an arm around his shoulder, stroking the hair on his chest with fingers that moved downward then and became more intimate. A bare leg slid over his hip. He rolled into her.

CHAPTER 29

The next week passed relatively unnoticed by the Detroit Police Department. There were no drug shootings, no blue babies found in trash cans, two rapes, three armed robberies, and only one arson attempt. The homicide rate rested. Blissfully the two city newspapers made no mention of the slack time, being careful not to seem to imply that the criminals weren't trying hard enough. The three local television stations noted the downturn, one of them expressing hope in an editorial by the general manager that the city had reached the turning point in its quest for respectability. That night someone was stabbed during basketball practice at Wayne State University, a junior high school teacher in Warren was arrested for having sex with three of his male students, and the owners of a mom-and-pop party store in Redford Township were shotgunned to death for $143.75 in the cash register and four cartons of Marlboros. Channel 7 sent a minicam crew to photograph the bloodstains. Inspector George Pontier of Detroit Homicide declined an interview.

The attempted arson had to do with a homemade bomb discovered between pews at the Reverend Sunsmith's church by a custodian. A timer wired to a small gelatin charge attached to a plastic five-gallon can of gasoline had failed to trigger an explosion. The Detroit Bomb Squad was summoned, headed by a lieutenant named Zangara, who grinned, patted the mechanism, and said, "Filzer, where you been keeping yourself?" He then defused the bomb with one snip of a pair of insulated wire cutters.

Michael Boniface and his companion, Carmine Picante, were questioned and released early in the week in connection with the kidnapping of the Reverend Thomas Aquinas Sunsmith. By that time the local media had begun to treat both the incident and the failed arson as publicity ploys by the flamboyant guitar player turned minister, and Boniface's role in the investigation received only passing mention. The *Free Press* referred to him as "a one-time prominent figure in the Detroit underworld." The *News* buried the item in the third section with a photograph taken when Boniface was imprisoned on the narcotics charge. The female newscaster who drew the story on Channel 2 mispronounced his name.

Toward the end of the week, the Reverend Sunsmith hosted a press conference to field rumors surrounding his disappearance, but it dissolved into a tent revival when one reporter's question sidetracked him onto the gambling measure. A cartoon in the *News* depicted the minister attempting to part the Detroit River using an umbrella riddled with holes for a staff. A more serious item analyzed the Detroit Police Department's refusal to stem the growing curiosity regarding the finances of the Reverend's church.

On Saturday, Charles Maggiore was released from Detroit Receiving Hospital. A statement was issued to the press some minutes after his wheelchair was escorted under plainclothes guard through a rear exit, where Gordy helped him into the big Lincoln and drove him home.

Gordy was helping him out of the car when a detective

sergeant named Stills stepped out from behind a hedge and showed Maggiore a warrant for his arrest. The charge was conspiracy to commit arson in collusion with one Howard Arnold Filzer, in custody.

"Police declined to say where Maggiore is being held," announced Channel 4's silver-haired anchorman. "He is recovering from wounds received in a suspected gangland attempt on his life and is believed to still be in danger."

Picante turned off the set in the living room of Michael Boniface's suite. "Cheap son of a bitch got what he paid for," he said.

"They better be giving Filzer the same protection. Get the ball, Al." Boniface tossed the green plastic sphere he had had Picante bring him from the gift shop in the lobby. The golden retriever, seated on the floor next to its master's chair, watched it bounce and roll to a stop in a corner, its bell jangling. Al made no move to follow.

"Stupid mutt," said Picante.

"He thinks it's silly. Don't you, boy?" He scratched under Al's chin. The dog closed its eyes and leaned against his knee. "Animals got a stronger sense of dignity than humans."

"I guess that's why they spend so much time licking their pricks."

"That fucking Maggiore," Boniface said, and Picante smiled at the juxtaposition. "He's smarter than any of us figured and dumber than any of us expected. He snatches the nigger and then cuts him loose so he can spread that dumb story and come off looking like a horse's ass. Got half the town thinking he went out shopping for headlines and the other half ready to swear he spent the time shacked up with a parishioner's wife. Then the fucking hunchback tries to torch the church just in case Sunsmith puts him to it and decides to roll over on him. Dumb."

"Still think the snatch was Maggiore's?"

"Hell, yes. He's the only one strapped enough to try it and the only one lucky enough to pull it off. I hate to see anyone shit on his luck like that, even him."

"Who's going to put the hit on him now we lost Macklin?"

"Macklin, I never thought he'd be the one to turn." He pushed the dog's head away. It got up, went over to the corner where the ball had come to rest, sniffed at it, and curled up on the carpet. "Forget Maggiore. He's past hitting now. If that gambling referendum ever had a chance of passing it's now. They'll vote it in just to dump all over Sunsmith. They're madder at him than they are at Maggiore, with or without the torching."

"Put the hit on Sunsmith."

"No. You don't hit cops or clergymen."

"Hit this one." Picante pulled a chair in front of Boniface's and sat down on the edge of the cushion, leaning forward. "He gets dead good and loud everyone will forget the kidnapping, figure the pro-gamblers took him out to shut him up. The referendum's Tuesday. We can still spike it, but we got to move fast. Sunsmith's holding a rally in Hart Plaza Monday. We'll hit him there."

"Shooter gets within twenty feet his bodyguards'll cut him to pieces."

"So we use two shooters."

Boniface said nothing. The lines in his face were pulled deep. He didn't look bloated now, just old.

Picante said, "The town's crawling with hungry buttons will throw themselves to the dogs if we put it to them right. While the guards are busy plugging the goat, our number two comes in from left field and hands the good Reverend his pie in the sky."

"You didn't just think of that."

"Mike, it's the only way. And it'll work."

"Maybe you already set it up." Boniface's tone was dead. "Maybe Maggiore's not the only one fixed to heel over. I'm next, maybe."

"Don't talk like that, Mike. I wanted your spot I'd of took it while you were inside."

"You wouldn't of been able to. You needed me out so you could use my name, make contacts."

"You don't believe that."

After a moment the lines softened. "Naw. Hell, no. Things are just different out here. You get scared, you ain't sure who's your friend. *Figlio mio.*" He reached out and patted Picante's accordioned cheek.

"*Mi padre.*" Picante grasped the old man's knee and squeezed. "What about Sunsmith?"

"Forget Sunsmith. I want you to call that Polack state senator we spent so much money on, whatsizname, Subasic, see can he stall this thing past November. It's too late to do anything about the vote Tuesday."

Picante's long face sobered. He withdrew his hand. "Sure, Mike. I'll call him today, start things moving."

"Take Al for a walk first."

"Okay."

"I'm bushed. Shake me up when you get in."

The day clerk in the Pontchartrain lobby was a bald man with a modest gray handlebar whose upturned points gave him a false look of good humor. He disapproved of the man in the ugly suit who was coming off the elevator and he disapproved of the dog he had on a leash. The hotel was strictly off limits to pets. But the man's employer had made a special financial arrangement with the manager that didn't include the day clerk.

"I'll be out for an hour," the man told him. "Mr. Boniface is resting. Don't disturb him."

"Yes, sir."

Outside, the wind was lifting skirts and blowing newspapers against pedestrians' legs. Al put his muzzle into the wind, eyes closed, nostrils quivering. Picante jerked the leash and the dog fell into step beside him.

The blue Mercury was parked on Washington. Picante

opened the rear door and Al hopped inside. He lowered the window two inches and closed the door on the dog, who whimpered and snuffled at the opening. Picante then opened the passenger's door in front, sat on the edge of the seat, and exchanged the Colt Diamondback under his left arm for a less expensive model in the glove compartment with its serial number gouged out. Ignoring Al's whining, he closed up and left the car and the dog.

He re-entered the hotel on the Jefferson side. Checkout time was noon and the lobby was jammed with guests and luggage and bellhops pushing wheeled carts. Picante climbed the fire stairs and waited inside the door on the seventh floor while a cleaning cart rattled past pulled by a maid. After a minute he opened the door a crack. The cart was parked outside the open door of one of the rooms. He took the long way around to 716, met no one on the way, and let himself inside with his key.

Boniface wasn't in the living room. Picante checked the bath, then went into the old man's bedroom. Boniface lay on his side on the bed in his shirtsleeves and stockinged feet, snoring gently.

Picante had carried a towel in with him from the bathroom. He unclipped the revolver from under his arm, wrapped the thick towel completely around it and his hand, and placed the bundle against Boniface's right temple. The sleeping man stirred.

Muffled by the towel, the report was no louder than the thud of a heavy book striking a carpeted floor. The old man jerked. Bits of fiber swirled around angrily, then floated down through air clouded with smoke and tainted with the stench of charred cloth. Boniface's bowels voided.

Picante wiped off the gun with the towel and placed both on the bed. Then he went out to finish walking the dog.

CHAPTER 30

Roger Macklin succumbed to temptation finally and called the suite.

He had heard from Picante twice in two days, the first time just after the news of the Reverend Sunsmith's kidnapping had broken, the second following his release. Both times Picante had told Roger to stand by for instructions. Then nothing. Now it was Friday afternoon, three days away from Sunsmith's rally, and the tension was getting to be like the old urgency when he had gone too long between fixes. That scared him and he dialed the number. After three rings a strange voice came on the line.

"Hello?"

Roger hung up. Picante always answered, "Yeah?" He wondered if Boniface had answered, and he supposed he'd catch hell for calling there. He hoped he hadn't blown his big opportunity.

Then that evening he had the radio on and learned that Boniface was dead, murdered in his suite, and that an associate of his was being questioned at Detroit Police Headquarters. That would be Picante. He knew then that the voice on the telephone had belonged to a police officer. He started daydreaming then, wondering how the job had gone down and how he'd have handled it. It was a few moments before he pieced things together and knew as well as if Picante had told him that Picante had killed his boss. And that made him worry, because if the police arrested him for the murder then there was no one to stand the contract on Sunsmith. He was thinking along these lines when his telephone rang.

"Roger? Me."

"Hey, they let you go?"

"Sure, what'd you expect?"

"Listen, I want to ask—"

"Save it. You all set?"

"Set?"

"You got all the stuff down, you want to go over it again, what?"

"You mean it's on?"

"You ever think it wouldn't be?"

"Well, after they arrested you."

"Nobody arrested anybody. You want to go over it again? 'Cause if you don't I got other things that need doing."

"No. No, I'm fine."

"Okay, then. I'll call you after." The line clicked and buzzed.

Pegging the receiver, Roger glimpsed his reflection in the window. "Treat us like mushrooms," he told it. "Keep us in the dark and throw shit on us."

"He did it okay. I guess I know a wrong one when I see him."

Sergeant Lovelady leaned his forehead against the grilled window in Pontier's office, looking down at Beaubien as if he expected to see Picante and the young lawyer who used to represent Michael Boniface coming out there. But the pair had been gone for an hour.

"All we get in here is wrong ones," Pontier said, seating himself on the edge of his cluttered desk with his hands in his pockets. "We know Maggiore had paper out on Boniface. Picante sure didn't set up that shotgunning in Belleville and then put himself in front of it next to his boss."

"It was damn considerate of the dog to have to take a leak just when the shooter was fixing to come in."

"Maybe the dog was in on it."

"Yeah, laugh. We know Boniface didn't hire Macklin to grab Sunsmith. Maybe Picante hired Macklin to off Boniface."

"And brought Boniface along to the zoo to witness the transaction?"

"Well, then that was something else and Picante did the burn himself. He was a heavyweight before he started picking up after the old man."

"Why blow down Boniface now? What's Picante got to gain from killing a racketeer without a racket? Arson's got Maggiore. Let's don't be greedy."

"Picante's running some game, I know it."

"Right now there's only one game in town." Pontier stopped.

Lovelady turned from the window. "We keep coming back to Sunsmith."

"We do." Pontier reached over and lifted the receiver off his telephone. "Tactical Mobile Unit still handling crowd control?"

"Last I heard."

He dialed a number, waited. "This is Pontier in Homicide. Who can I talk to about security at Hart Plaza next Monday?"

Macklin despised inertia, for the simple reason that he was so susceptible to it.

Activity was his aphrodisiac, and although he had the kind of features that always looked tired, he seldom was.

Long periods of inaction, however, were fatal, enforcing a cataleptic lethargy that in recent years had become steadily more difficult to throw off. By the end of his week in hiding at Carmen Thalberg's house he was sleeping fifteen hours a day. But his sleep was light, and when the late edition of the *News* hit the front door he heard the thump. He rose and dressed and was tying his shoelaces when Carmen came in carrying the newspaper.

"Did you know him?" She unfolded it and held it out.

Macklin's eyes landed first on the photograph of a bagged corpse being slid into an ambulance parked on Washington. Then he read the caption. He snatched the newspaper from her.

She said, "I thought you might. Does it have anything to do with you?"

He read all of the article that appeared on page one and put it down without turning to the inside page where it was continued. He looked around. Carmen went over to the bedstand and took his magnum and belt holster out of the drawer. He accepted them, slid the gun out, and checked the load. Then he sheathed it and snapped the holster onto his belt under his jacket.

"You're going out? What about the police?"

"I have to find my son."

"Your son?"

"I think the man who killed Boniface is going to kill him. Or get him killed. It's the same thing."

She looked at him. He grasped her shoulder. She was wearing a cream silk blouse and his fingers crushed the material. "You asked me once if I ever did anything for someone's life. I'm going to try."

"Is his worth it?"

"Maybe not. And maybe I don't have a choice either way." He let go of her.

"I'll go with you."

"No. If I know Pontier he's got officers watching this place. You'll have to draw them off. They'll follow you."

"What are you going to do?"

He grinned. There was no humor in it. "Lady, if I knew that I wouldn't be in such a hurry."

She kissed him hard. He was surprised into responding. After a long moment she pushed them apart.

"I don't love you," she said. "I just don't have a choice either way."

"We both have a problem," he said, and kissed her. Then she left.

CHAPTER 31

Donna, Macklin's ex-wife, was living with an oral surgeon named Riordan in Sterling Heights. After Carmen had driven away towing her police escort, Macklin took his car out of her garage and drove to a public telephone, where he got the number from Directory Assistance. Donna didn't want to come to the telephone at first and he had to communicate with her through Riordan until she came on and told him she hadn't heard from Roger in months. The last time she had tried to call him at his old apartment she had been informed that he had moved out without leaving a forwarding address. Macklin hung up on her questions and tried an acquaintance in the Detroit Police Department, Armed Robbery detail. The officer, wounded once in the line of duty and twice decorated for heroism by the commissioner, moonlighted as a contract killer for the Rubello family in Grosse Pointe. He told Macklin he'd get back to him. Macklin replied that he'd call back and stopped talking to him after receiving a warning that the pick-up order on him was still in force.

He called old Hermann's house and reached the housekeeper, who explained in broken English that her employer was in Las Vegas. By then he had run out of change for the telephone. He got back into the car and took Telegraph south into Detroit, where he attracted the attention of a city blue-and-white, which followed him for two blocks until he caught a light on the yellow and lost him. He was pretty sure the officer hadn't gotten close enough to read his license plate or he'd have turned on his siren and run the light. Macklin left Telegraph then and wound his way down through side streets.

He garaged the Camaro on Clairmount and walked to a cave of a bar run by a former Red Wing goalie named Veauxhill, who had been thrown out of the league for gambling and had invested his winnings in the bar and a loan-sharking operation in back. A black bartender with a glass eye went into the back when Macklin asked for Veauxhill and returned a minute later, jerking his head toward the doorway he had just come through. Macklin went around the bar and through the opening.

Veauxhill was sitting at the folding card table he used for a desk, counting hundred-dollar bills into stacks on the red vinyl surface. A square man running to hard fat, he had a head the size of a pumpkin growing straight up out of a green silk bowling shirt and glistening black hair that showed the marks of the comb. His mouth was small and lipless and V-shaped, like the flap of an envelope, and his nose was a blister with nostrils, the bridge smashed flat by a hockey stick years before. His broken-knuckled hands were astonishingly swift and graceful as he counted the bills from one to the other faster than the eye could follow.

"You like indy work?" he asked without looking up.

Macklin said, "It's the same work. I just get to pick and choose who I do it for now."

"I ain't hiring. I do my own collecting."

"I'm not looking for a job."

"Street talk says you're smoking. I know half a dozen snitches would turn you in for what the cops are offering. You know what it takes to make a grifter roll over on a mechanic."

"I'm not looking for a safe house either."

Veauxhill finished counting, snapped a thick rubber band around the last stack, and began transferring the stacks into a Dewar's carton on the floor next to his chair. "You pay the same vig as everybody else. I don't play favorites even with shooters."

"I don't need a loan. I'm looking for my son."

"He ain't been in."

"Would you know him if you saw him?"

"Until you brought him up I didn't know you had a son. I thought you heavyweights did all your fucking with your guns."

"You know him. Or of him. His name's Roger. He's been working for Maggiore."

The loan shark closed the flaps on the carton. "I hear some kid's been jerking chains for the hunchback. Maybe I hear he's your boy. My memory ain't what it was. You bounce enough pucks off your skull maybe yours wouldn't be either." He turned flat colorless eyes on Macklin for the first time.

Macklin had eighty thousand dollars sewn into the lining of his corduroy jacket and in his wallet. He separated ten hundred-dollar bills from the wallet and laid them out individually across the card table.

"He was shacking up with some dark meat in Dearborn Heights until she tried croaking herself a couple-three weeks ago." Veauxhill started stacking the bills. "Apartment complex on Dudley. She was a singer in Sunsmith's choir."

"I remember it. Where'd you hear this?"

"I got clients all over. They can't pay right now, they supply me with information."

"That brings us up to a couple of weeks ago."

"Maybe you came here with something more current."

"It better come to something."

Veauxhill's envelope-flap mouth formed a bland smile. "I got pancreas cancer. Best estimate I got so far is three months. You want to save me the sack time in ICU, you know where to find me."

Macklin said, "I need a car. Mine's on a sheet."

The shark sat back and fanned himself with the stack of bills. Macklin counted out another thousand, emptying his wallet.

"A-1 Rentals on Livernois. Ask for Peterson and use my name. Cash, no paperwork."

Macklin watched him arranging the fresh bills. "What are they going to do, bury two boxes?"

"You do what you do till you stop. You don't just sit around and wait."

The car was a black-and-tan Renault with a brake light that stuck on and drained the battery if he parked it and turned off the engine without pumping the brake. When he returned to it after placing an unsuccessful call from a drugstore to his man in Armed Robbery he ground the battery down the rest of the way trying to start the engine and had to wait half an hour for it to recharge itself. The car had cost him fifteen hundred dollars not counting the thousand he had paid Veauxhill.

The Dearborn Heights apartment complex was U-shaped, built of bricks laid in blocks that had then been set one atop another by a crane. The balconies were decorative, the rubber plants on either side of the entrance made of plastic. Macklin pressed the button labeled MANAGER and was surprised to learn that it rang.

On the other side of the glass security entrance, the door to an apartment opened, revealing a barrel body in a green quilted housedress. Something buzzed and Macklin opened the glass door. The woman peered at him through a crooked pair of glasses with a Band-Aid around one bow. She was black and wore a blonde pageboy wig that made her look like a gross Buster Brown. She appeared to be in her early sixties. "Yes?"

"I'm a friend of Sister Mercer's. Is she still living here?"

"She's in New Orleans with her folks."

"She moved?" He let his lips part. "When?"

"Right after she tried hanging herself." Imparting the news seemed to delight her. "Got herself mixed up with some white boy. God meant that he wouldn't of made us different colors. *You're* white." She adjusted her glasses, making sure.

"Would her friend be named Roger? Roger Macklin?"

"Roger's right. I don't know about the Macklin part. You ain't with that church of hers?"

"No. We used to be neighbors. I heard she was living here. I'm between planes and I thought I'd visit. Would you know where Roger is living?"

"That's the devil's church she was mixed up with. That rev'rund of hers wants to take away the numbers, keep the poor folks from bettering theirselves. He's the devil all right, and a commie to boot."

"Do you have a number or an address for Mercer in New Orleans?"

"The little bitch never told me nothing, God save her. If she did I could of told her there wouldn't be nothing but hell in it for her. I don't know where neither of them is."

"Would one of her neighbors know, do you think?"

"They wouldn't have nothing to do with her. Not the black folks, and surely not the whites. That rev'run, he come here hisself when she strung herself up, all trapped out like a downtown pimp. I seen the devil in his black eyes. I played the number 666 that day, you bet. It didn't come in." She sounded affronted.

Macklin thanked her and withdrew.

Around eleven P.M. he took a room in a retirement hotel

on Dubois run by a doctor who had lost his license for failing to report treatment of gunshot wounds suffered by local drug traffickers during the war with the Colombians. The doctor recognized him and charged him five hundred dollars for two nights. The room consisted of a single bed, a cracked bureau, and a painted-over window on a corner of the ground floor that had been occupied until recently by the janitor. Macklin used the telephone in the lobby to call police headquarters again, but was told that his acquaintance had gone home. He returned to his room, transferred another thousand dollars to his wallet, and used a needle and thread he had bought in a convenience store to restitch the lining containing the remaining seventy-five thousand.

He couldn't sleep. The catatonia was off now and all those needless hours of rest were backing up on him. At one o'clock he rose and searched the room for something to read. But the only book there was a scuffed Gideon Bible holding up a short leg of the bureau. He pulled it free, easing down the leg to avoid waking the household, and got back into bed with the Bible. He read Genesis from start to finish and found himself wondering what sort of weapon Cain had used to slay Abel. He drifted off finally around three-thirty.

The doctor rented him bathroom privileges and a razor the next morning. Freshened and shaved, he used the telephone again. The voice he spoke to at police headquarters informed him that his contact was off duty Saturday.

He stayed in most of the day, going out only once, to pick up a sack of hamburgers at a White Castle six blocks over and a paperback spy thriller at a drugstore on Brush. The doctor had offered to send someone to do these things for a fee, but Macklin declined. He ate the hamburgers and read the entire novel stretched out on the bed on top of the covers. It was full of foreign agents who spoke English, only the reader was supposed to believe they were actually speaking French and German and Russian, and ran around shooting one another from a mile away with high-powered rifles.

Macklin supposed he was in a rut.

Sunday his police acquaintance called. There was nothing in Records on Roger Macklin.

CHAPTER 32

Monday morning it rained, one of those icy slanting pavement-pounders that turned the downtown expressways into canals and caused furnaces to kick in all over the city. It swept across the skyline like a massive streetsweeper from west to east, raising steam from sidewalks warmed by an unsuspecting dawn, stitched the surface of Lake St. Clair, and blew out over Canada. By noon the sun had returned to dry Hart Plaza's sunken concrete surface in patches. Cobo Hall and Ford Auditorium and the poker-chip towers of the Renaissance Center looked shining and new.

The band hired by the Reverend Sunsmith—lead guitar, backup, bass, drums, and organ—struck up shortly thereafter, interspersing some mild punk with "My Sweet Lord," "Amazing Grace," "Day by Day," and "Jesus Christ Superstar." Spectators began filtering in in singles, pairs, and groups, and by the time the choir took up their positions in the recessed circle reserved for live entertainment, the plaza was filled. Sister Asaul, who had turned down a recording contract from Columbia to stay with the Reverend, soloed "The Old Rugged Cross" while the others hummed accompaniment, their yellow satin robes shimmering under the high sun. A soprano provided by a local booking agent sang in place of Sister Mercer, who was still in New Orleans, recovering from her suicide attempt. TV cameras recorded details.

Sunsmith appeared at two o'clock, parting the crowd from the Jefferson Avenue side inside a flying wedge made up of the elders, a splash of bright rose ringed in blue. Three of the bodyguards were new, on loan from a security firm in Clawson. The band hurled itself into "Saviour, Like a Shepherd Lead Us." The choir sang. Some of those in the crowd joined in. As the five men swept toward the pulpit erected in front of the sisters, the mouth of the bodyguard walking point was moving, but not in time to the music.

Pontier stood with his back to Jefferson, feeling foolish in the tan raincoat he had slipped into before coming there. At that time the sky had still been threatening. But the left slash pocket was useful for concealing his walking radio. In the shifting of the crowd before the men approaching the pulpit he glimpsed a flash of yellow sportcoat. He drew out the radio. "Lovelady?"

"Yeah." The sergeant's voice wheezed out of the tiny speaker.

"Who's got Sunsmith's back?"

"Anderson and Cletus. Rubio's on the roof of Cobo with a sniperscope."

"See if you can get some more uniforms close to the middle. Stop any shooting before it starts."

"Dream on, Inspector."

"Yeah. Hey, what's that blue suit in front saying?"

" 'Get out of my way or I'll kill you.' "

On "Thou hast loved us," the music stopped, allowing Sister Asaul's rich mezzo-soprano to intone "love us still" into a dramatic silence. It was still reverberating when the

Reverend mounted to the pulpit behind the bulletproof plastic shield rising above it. He opened the rose-colored Bible he had carried in while the four elders took up their stance on his other side from the sisters. The pages crackled in the charged air, then stopped. The black eyes raked the assembly.

" 'For many deceivers are entered into the world,' wrote John, 'who confess not that Jesus Christ is come in the flesh. This is a deceiver and an antichrist.' "

His voice was strangely subdued, not the booming baritone that hummed along the rafters of his church. As the crowd pressed in to hear his words, Picante moved toward the left, near the choir and away from the bodyguards.

" 'Whosoever transgresseth, and abideth not in the doctrine of Christ, hath not God. He that abideth in the doctrine of Christ, he hath both the Father and the Son.' "

Macklin hurried across Jefferson, toward the murmur of Sunsmith's voice. He had not reckoned on the amount of traffic coming in for the rally and had finally left the rented Renault at a stoplight on Monroe. The horns of the automobiles stranded behind it were fading now. His clothes were showing signs of not having been changed in three days and he was unshaven. There had been no razor available in the Dearborn motel room where he had spent last night. The doctor in the retirement hotel on Dubois had refused to rent him the janitor's room for a third night.

Too late he spotted Inspector Pontier's bald head on the edge of the crowd. Their eyes met for an instant before Macklin slid in among the bodies.

" 'If there come any unto you, and bring not this doctrine, receive him not into your house, neither bid him God speed.' "

"Macklin's here!" Pontier barked into the radio. "Heading your way."

Lovelady said, "I don't see him."

"Collier, this is Pontier. Get some asses moving. Clear the plaza."

"Who died and elected you President?" A thin voice, strung tight, twanged out of the speaker. "Security's my lookout."

"Then start looking out. We got a known shooter in the crowd. Male cauc, six feet and one-eighty-five, black and gray, about forty, gray coat."

"Jesus Christ. All units, this is Lieutenant Collier. Clear everybody out. We got a shooter."

" 'For he that biddeth him God speed is partaker of his evil deeds.' "

For the first time since he had received the Call, the Reverend Thomas Aquinas Sunsmith was losing his audience. Whistles were blowing and the crowd was surging away from him, being poked and prodded by police officers in uniform and men waving black radios. He abandoned his text, stepping around in front of the pulpit and waving his arms, shouting that the Philistines were trying to prevent them from hearing the Word.

One figure was moving against the tide. Macklin recognized Roger's gait before he recognized his son's features, the loose-limbed stride and his own forward-leaning posture. A breeze caught the boy's long black hair, straightening it behind him. He was reaching inside the front of his tan Windbreaker as he neared the pulpit, threading his way between the heaving bodies.

"Roger!"

The shout was smothered under shrieking whistles and raised voices. Macklin shouldered his way toward his son. An officer stepped into his path and Macklin threw an elbow into the man's face, feeling his nose collapse. The officer melted away before him. He pushed forward, reaching under his coat for the magnum. He had already spotted Picante near the pulpit, saw his hand going under his left arm.

The elders saw the youth approaching with his hand inside his jacket. The 9-millimeter semiautomatics came out.

"Roger!"

That time Roger heard him. Macklin saw his head turning in his direction. The elders saw it too and held their fire. Then the boy's head swung back. He hadn't seen his father in the crowd.

Macklin shouted again. The magnum caught the sunlight. The flash caught the attention of the elders, who swung their guns around. Macklin saw the smoke coming out of the barrels in round puffs. He was struck by bowling balls. He felt himself pitching forward, saw the concrete come up.

Picante, on a level with the pulpit now, stuck his Colt Diamondback into the Reverend's robes and squeezed the trigger three times. Sunsmith shuddered. Blood came out of his mouth and skidded down the rose-colored satin.

Picante jerked backward off the platform and landed hard on his back with his arms flung wide, a crucifix in doubleknits with scarlet spreading on his shirtfront and a startled look on his long face. An instant later came the report from the roof of Cobo Hall overlooking Jefferson, its echo retreating toward Windsor.

The crowd was panicking now, pitching in a writhing mass toward the open. Roger was caught up in the tide. He took his hand out of his Windbreaker empty and turned and let the crowd carry him away from the pulpit, out of Hart Plaza. He hadn't seen either Sunsmith or Picante fall or whom the bodyguards had been shooting at. His first thought was that a lot of people were mad at the Reverend.

One of the elders crouched with Sunsmith's huge head in his lap. The black eyes were open, moist black candle drippings. The other bodyguards stood looking down at him with their guns at their sides lisping smoke. One of the sisters was wailing. Sister Asaul recited the Lord's Prayer.

Macklin lay on his side on the concrete. He had been kicked a number of times and his hand had been stepped on.

but the shouting and shuffling were receding now. Out of the corner of his eye he saw men in uniform coming with revolvers in their hands, glimpsed Inspector Pontier's bald head and a fat man in a yellow coat whose name he couldn't remember. He smelled concrete and blood and spent powder, and as the noise of the crowd died away he thought he could hear the Detroit River lapping the bank. All of his senses seemed abnormally acute.

"Macklin." The man's head and shoulders were lost in the sun's glare, but Macklin recognized Pontier's voice. He didn't respond. His mouth felt as if it were full of saliva.

"Forget it." This was the fat man.

"Shit," said Macklin then. "I was going to say the same thing."

The nurse who undressed him at Receiving wondered about the crackling in his riddled coat and found the lining quilted with hundred-dollar bills, some of them bullet-torn and all of them clotted with gore. This discovery was unknown to Dr. Stepp, then swiftly but half-heartedly scrubbing for the emergency operation. He'd rather be in his office drafting the paper he planned to submit to the *Harvard Medical Journal*. Gunshot wounds weren't nearly as interesting as a patient with his own unborn twin grafted onto his left shoulder.

MORE MYSTERIOUS PLEASURES

HAROLD ADAMS

MURDER

Carl Wilcox debuts in a story of triple murder which exposes the underbelly of corruption in the town of Corden, shattering the respectability of its most dignified citizens. #501 $3.50

THE NAKED LIAR

When a sexy young widow is framed for the murder of her husband, Carl Wilcox comes through to help her fight off cops and big-city goons. #420 $3.95

THE FOURTH WIDOW

Ex-con/private eye Carl Wilcox is back, investigating the death of a "popular" widow in the Depression-era town of Corden, S.D. #502 $3.50

EARL DERR BIGGERS

THE HOUSE WITHOUT A KEY

Charlie Chan debuts in the Honolulu investigation of an expatriate Bostonian's murder. #421 $3.95

THE CHINESE PARROT

Charlie Chan works to find the key to murders seemingly without victims—but which have left a multitude of clues. #503 $3.95

BEHIND THAT CURTAIN

Two murders sixteen years apart, one in London, one in San Francisco, each share a major clue in a pair of velvet Chinese slippers. Chan seeks the connection. #504 $3.95

THE BLACK CAMEL

When movie goddess Sheila Fane is murdered in her Hawaiian pavilion, Chan discovers an interrelated crime in a murky Hollywood mystery from the past. #505 $3.95

CHARLIE CHAN CARRIES ON

An elusive transcontinental killer dogs the heels of the Lofton Round the World Cruise. When the touring party reaches Honolulu, the murderer finally meets his match. #506 $3.95

JOE GORES

A TIME OF PREDATORS

When Paula Halstead kills herself after witnessing a horrid crime, her husband vows to avenge her death. Winner of the Edgar Allan Poe Award.
#215 $3.95

COME MORNING

Two million in diamonds are at stake, and the ex-con who knows their whereabouts may have trouble staying alive if he turns them up at the wrong moment.
#518 $3.95

NAT HENTOFF

BLUES FOR CHARLIE DARWIN

Gritty, colorful Greenwich Village sets the scene for Noah Green and Sam McKibbon, two street-wise New York cops who are as at home in jazz clubs as they are at a homicide scene.
#208 $3.95

THE MAN FROM INTERNAL AFFAIRS

Detective Noah Green wants to know who's stuffing corpses into East Village garbage cans . . . and who's lying about him to the Internal Affairs Division.
#409 $3.95

PATRICIA HIGHSMITH

THE BLUNDERER

An unhappy husband attempts to kill his wife by applying the murderous methods of another man. When things go wrong, he pays a visit to the more successful killer—a dreadful error.
#305 $3.95

DOUG HORNIG

THE DARK SIDE

Insurance detective Loren Swift is called to a rural commune to investigate a carbon-monoxide murder. Are the commune inhabitants as gentle as they seem?
#519 $3.95

P.D. JAMES/T.A. CRITCHLEY

THE MAUL AND THE PEAR TREE

The noted mystery novelist teams up with a police historian to create a fascinating factual account of the 1811 Ratcliffe Highway murders.
#520 $3.95

STUART KAMINSKY'S "TOBY PETERS" SERIES

NEVER CROSS A VAMPIRE

When Bela Lugosi receives a dead bat in the mail, Toby tries to catch the prankster. But Toby's time is at a premium because he's also trying to clear William Faulkner of a murder charge!
#107 $3.95

HIGH MIDNIGHT
When Gary Cooper and Ernest Hemingway come to Toby for protection, he tries to save them from vicious blackmailers. #106 $3.95

HE DONE HER WRONG
Someone has stolen Mae West's autobiography, and when she asks Toby to come up and see her sometime, he doesn't know how deadly a visit it could be. #105 $3.95

BULLET FOR A STAR
Warner Brothers hires Toby Peters to clear the name of Errol Flynn, a blackmail victim with a penchant for young girls. The first novel in the acclaimed Hollywood-based private eye series. #308 $3.95

THE FALA FACTOR
Toby comes to the rescue of lady-in-distress Eleanor Roosevelt, and must match wits with a right-wing fanatic who is scheming to overthrow the U.S. Government. #309 $3.95

JOSEPH KOENIG

FLOATER
Florida Everglades sheriff Buck White matches wits with a Miami murder-and-larceny team who just may have hidden his ex-wife's corpse in a remote bayou. #521 $3.50

ELMORE LEONARD

THE HUNTED
Long out of print, this 1974 novel by the author of *Glitz* details the attempts of a man to escape killers from his past. #401 $3.95

MR. MAJESTYK
Sometimes bad guys can push a good man too far, and when that good guy is a Special Forces veteran, everyone had better duck. #402 $3.95

THE BIG BOUNCE
Suspense and black comedy are cleverly combined in this tale of a dangerous drifter's affair with a beautiful woman out for kicks. #403 $3.95

ELSA LEWIN

I, ANNA
A recently divorced woman commits murder to avengé her degradation at the hands of a sleazy lothario. #522 $3.50

THOMAS MAXWELL

KISS ME ONCE
An epic *roman noir* which explores the romantic but seamy underworld of New York during the WWII years. When the good guys are off fighting in Europe, the bad guys run amok in America. #523 $3.95

PATRICK RUELL

RED CHRISTMAS

Murderers and political terrorists come down the chimney during an old-fashioned Dickensian Christmas at a British country inn.

#531 $3.50

DEATH TAKES THE LOW ROAD

William Hazlitt, a universtiy administrator who moonlights as a Soviet mole, is on the run from both Russian and British agents who want him to assassinate an African general. #532 $3.50

DELL SHANNON

CASE PENDING

In the first novel in the best-selling series, Lt. Luis Mendoza must solve a series of horrifying Los Angeles mutilation murders. #211 $3.95

THE ACE OF SPADES

When the police find an overdosed junkie, they're ready to write off the case—until the autopsy reveals that this junkie *wasn't* a junkie. #212 $3.95

EXTRA KILL

In "The Temple of Mystic Truth," Mendoza discovers idol worship, pornography, murder, and the clue to the death of a Los Angeles patrolman. #213 $3.95

KNAVE OF HEARTS

Mendoza must clear the name of the L.A.P.D. when it's discovered that an innocent man has been executed and the real killer is still on the loose. #214 $3.95

DEATH OF A BUSYBODY

When the West Coast's most industrious gossip and meddler turns up dead in a freight yard, Mendoza must work without clues to find the killer of a woman who had offended nearly everyone in Los Angeles. #315 $3.95

DOUBLE BLUFF

Mendoza goes against the evidence to dissect what looks like an air-tight case against suspected wife-killer Francis Ingram—a man the lieutenant insists is too nice to be a murderer. #316 $3.95

MARK OF MURDER

Mendoza investigates the near-fatal attack on an old friend as well as trying to track down an insane serial killer. #417 $3.95

ROOT OF ALL EVIL

The murder of a "nice" girl leads Mendoza to team up with the FBI in the search for her not-so-nice boyfriend—a Soviet agent. #418 $3.95

JULIE SMITH

TRUE-LIFE ADVENTURE

Paul McDonald earned a meager living ghosting reports for a San Francisco private eye until the gumshoe turned up dead . . . now the killers are after him. #407 $3.95

TOURIST TRAP

A lunatic is out to destroy San Francisco's tourism industry; can feisty lawyer/sleuth Rebecca Schwartz stop him while clearing an innocent man of a murder charge? #533 $3.95

ROSS H. SPENCER

THE MISSING BISHOP

Chicago P.I. Buzz Deckard has a missing person to find. Unfortunately his client has disappeared as well, and no one else seems to be who or what they claim. #416 $3.50

MONASTERY NIGHTMARE

Chicago P.I. Luke Lassiter tries his hand at writing novels, and encounters murder in an abandoned monastery. #534 $3.50

REX STOUT

UNDER THE ANDES

A long-lost 1914 fantasy novel from the creator of the immortal Nero Wolfe series. "The most exciting yarn we have read since *Tarzan of the Apes.*"—*All-Story Magazine.* #419 $3.50

ROSS THOMAS

CAST A YELLOW SHADOW

McCorkle's wife is kidnapped by agents of the South African government. The ransom—his cohort Padillo must assassinate their prime minister. #535 $3.95

THE SINGAPORE WINK

Ex-Hollywood stunt man Ed Cauthorne is offered $25,000 to search for colleague Angelo Sacchetti—a man he thought he'd killed in Singapore two years earlier. #536 $3.95

THE FOOLS IN TOWN ARE ON OUR SIDE

Lucifer Dye, just resigned from a top secret U.S. Intelligence post, accepts a princely fee to undertake the corruption of an entire American city. #537 $3.95

JIM THOMPSON

THE KILL-OFF

Luanne Devore was loathed by everyone in her small New England town. Her plots and designs threatened to destroy them—unless they destroyed her first. #538 $3.95

DAVID WILLIAMS' "MARK TREASURE" SERIES

UNHOLY WRIT

London financier Mark Treasure helps a friend reaquire some property. He stays to unravel the mystery when a Shakespeare manuscript is discovered and foul murder done. #112 $3.95

TREASURE BY DEGREES

Mark Treasure discovers there's nothing funny about a board game called "Funny Farms." When he becomes involved in the takeover struggle for a small university, he also finds there's nothing funny about murder. #113 $3.95

AVAILABLE AT YOUR BOOKSTORE OR DIRECT FROM THE PUBLISHER

Mysterious Press Mail Order
129 West 56th Street
New York, NY 10019

Please send me the MYSTERIOUS PRESS titles I have circled below:

103 105 106 107 112 113 208 209 210 211 212 213
214 215 216 217 218 219 220 301 302 303 304 305
306 308 309 315 316 401 402 403 404 405 406 407
408 409 410 411 412 413 414 415 416 417 418 419
420 421 501 502 503 504 505 506 507 508 509 510
511 512 513 514 515 516 517 518 519 520 521 522
523 524 525 526 527 528 529 530 531 532 533 534
535 536 537 538 539 540 541 542 543 544 545

I am enclosing $ ______________ (please add $2.00 postage and handling for the first book, and 25¢ for each additional book). Send check or money order only—no cash or C.O.D.'s please. Allow at least 4 weeks for delivery.

NAME ______________________________

ADDRESS ______________________________

CITY ______________ STATE __________ ZIP CODE __________

New York State residents please add appropriate sales tax.

Add some mystery to your life with

THE ARMCHAIR DETECTIVE

This award winning quarterly is now in its 19th year as the mystery world's most distinguished critical journal. Each issue is profusely illustrated and has 112 pages of interviews, in-depth articles, bibliographies, and enough book reviews to satisfy the most insatiable mystery fan. Don't let the mystery world be a mystery to you—subscribe now! One year—$20. Sample copy—$6.

☐ 1 year (4 issues), $20
☐ 2 years (8 issues), $36
☐ Sample copy $6
☐ New subscription
☐ Gift

☐ Outside U.S.A., 1 year $24 (surface mail)
☐ Outside U.S.A., 2 years $44 (surface mail)
☐ Outside U.S.A., 1 year $36 (air mail)
☐ Outside U.S.A., 2 years $66 (air mail)

PLEASE PRINT

Name ____________________

Address ____________________

City ____________ State ________ Zip ________

ALSO, PLEASE SEND TAD TO THE FOLLOWING FOR ONE YEAR (4 ISSUES)

Name ____________________

Address ____________________

City ____________ State ________ Zip ________

The Armchair Detective 129 West 56th Street
New York, N.Y. 10019 (212) 765-0900